"Matteo?"

The way Mari said his name turned the heat to scorching hot. He couldn't even be sure which one of them moved first. But in the next instant their lips were joined.

Matteo thrust his hands through her hair, pulling her closer. He'd never be able to get her close enough. Never be able to get enough of the way she tasted, felt against the length of his body.

Finally, a small voice of reason cried out in the back recesses of his brain. Though it would be so easy to continue kissing her, tasting her, pulling her ever so closer to him, Matteo knew he had to stop.

This wasn't the time or the place. With more strength than he would have guessed he possessed, he reluctantly let her go.

Dear Reader,

Holidays and vacations always come to an end much too soon, don't they? But imagine having the kind of job that has you living in a luxurious resort year-round. Mariana Renati happens to have just such a position on the lovely island of Sardinia, Italy. She's worked hard to get to where she is and continues to put in long hours with a heavy workload to make sure her guests are well taken care of. But one day Matteo Talarico shows up and questions her abilities, her very right to be where she is.

To add further turmoil to her life, she's attracted to him in a way she cannot ignore.

For his part, Matteo has his reasons to be suspicious of Mari. He's seen firsthand how trusting the wrong person can ruin someone's life. But the more he gets to know her, the harder it is to see her as anything less than what she is—someone competent and honorable who deserves everything she's worked so hard to achieve. She's also the woman he can't live without.

I hope you enjoy the journey that takes them from rivals to lovers.

Nina

RESISTING HIS CINDERELLA RIVAL

NINA SINGH

ROMANCE

If you purchased this book without a cover you should be aware that this book is stolen property. It was reported as "unsold and destroyed" to the publisher, and neither the author nor the publisher has received any payment for this "stripped book."

ISBN-13: 978-1-335-47053-9

Recycling programs for this product may not exist in your area.

Resisting His Cinderella Rival

Copyright © 2025 by Nilay Nina Singh

All rights reserved. No part of this book may be used or reproduced in any manner whatsoever without written permission.

Without limiting the author's and publisher's exclusive rights, any unauthorized use of this publication to train generative artificial intelligence (AI) technologies is expressly prohibited.

This is a work of fiction. Names, characters, places and incidents are either the product of the author's imagination or are used fictitiously. Any resemblance to actual persons, living or dead, businesses, companies, events or locales is entirely coincidental.

For questions and comments about the quality of this book, please contact us at CustomerService@Harlequin.com.

TM and ® are trademarks of Harlequin Enterprises ULC.

Harlequin Enterprises ULC
22 Adelaide St. West, 41st Floor
Toronto, Ontario M5H 4E3, Canada
www.Harlequin.com

Printed in U.S.A.

Nina Singh lives just outside Boston, Massachusetts, with her husband, children and a very rambunctious Yorkie. After several years in the corporate world, she finally followed the advice of family and friends to "give the writing a go, already." She's oh-so happy she did. When not at her keyboard, she likes to spend time on the tennis court or golf course. Or immersed in a good read.

Books by Nina Singh

Harlequin Romance

A Five-Star Family Reunion

Wearing His Ring till Christmas

How to Make a Wedding

From Tropical Fling to Forever

If the Fairy Tale Fits...

Part of His Royal World

Winter Escapes

Prince's Proposal for the Canadian Cameras

Whisked into the Billionaire's World
Caribbean Contract with Her Boss
Two Weeks to Tempt the Tycoon
The Prince's Safari Temptation
Their Accidental Marriage Deal
Bound by the Boss's Baby

Visit the Author Profile page
at Harlequin.com for more titles.

For my children. For taking me to places
I would never think to go.

**Praise for
Nina Singh**

"A captivating holiday adventure!
Their Festive Island Escape by Nina Singh is a twist
on an enemies-to-lovers trope and is sure to delight.
I recommend this book to anyone.... It's fun,
it's touching and it's satisfying."
—*Goodreads*

CHAPTER ONE

HE WAS GOING to have to start all over. From square one.

Matteo Talarico slammed his laptop shut and stared at the Roman skyline outside his window. The Emmanuel Monument stood magnificently tall and grand against the setting sun in the horizon. A year ago, he would have never guessed that he'd have to give up looking at that view. Give up the office and the building that held it.

It was gone. All of it. Liquidated. The family's holdings set up on the auction block like discarded remains. After all these years, it had taken one man's folly to bring it all down. That man being his father.

Stefan Talarico had ruined the business his own father, Matteo's grandfather, had started and nurtured all those years ago. To make matters worse, he'd done so in the most clichéd way imaginable.

He'd let himself be duped by a beautiful woman.

Like a true mark, his old man had fallen for the false compliments and pretty—ultimately fake—platitudes simply because they'd been uttered through pretty, pouty lips.

Matteo rubbed his forehead and tried to clear his head. The negative and angry thoughts churning through his head for the past couple of years, ever since that woman had entered his father's life, did nothing to better the reality he was facing. Decades of consistent business growth and success only to have it end with such chaos and loss.

Tala Industries, a name synonymous with high-end luxury condominiums and deluxe commercial real estate, was on the brink of complete bankruptcy.

Whatever it took, he would see the woman pay for what she'd done. If he could ever find her.

First things first, Matteo had to come up with a plan to rebuild Tala Industries from the ground up. One brick at a time. If only he knew where to start.

His cell phone vibrated on the desk behind him and he groaned. He was getting so tired of answering calls from creditors and business scavengers alike. But the contact that appeared on his screen told him that the call was from neither. Though probably not all that much better.

He clicked on the icon to answer his lawyer's call. "Aldo. Please tell me you're calling with some good news," he said, though that was highly unlikely and they both knew it.

"Well, in a sense, I think I might be."

Now that was curious. "In a sense?"

"My office received a call earlier this morning pertaining to you. From the islands."

"Which one?"

"Sardinia. Cagliari to be more precise."

Matteo wracked his brain but came up with nothing in response to the news. He didn't know anyone in the town of Cagliari. Or in any part of Sardinia, for that matter. He could count on one hand all the times he'd visited the Italian island south of the region of Tuscany. "And?"

"It turns out you had a distant relative who made her home there. An elderly distant cousin. On your mother's side."

The other man's use of the past tense told him whoever this great distant cousin had been, she was now gone. But what did it have to do with him? Aldo seemed to be taking his sweet time getting to the point. "Go on," Matteo prompted.

"She passed on last month. At the youthful age of ninety-eight. She didn't have any direct family of her own, it turns out. But apparently often talked fondly of a little tyke who visited her once or twice decades ago."

Huh. Matteo had zero recollection of any such visits. Though that wasn't surprising. His parents traipsed all over the Italian landscape when he was growing up, occasionally bringing him along. More often, they left him behind with the household staff.

Aldo continued, "She listed you as an inheritor of part of her estate. An estate attorney from a small office in Cagliari notified us that we'll be receiving the paperwork later this week."

He knew better than to get his hopes up in response to this unexpected news. After all, what kind of inheritance could a long-lost spinster cousin of his beloved mother possibly be able to afford him? In all likelihood, this phone call was probably just going to result in yet one more nuisance to-do item added to his already chaotic life presently. She'd likely left him knickknacks and collectibles he'd have to try and figure out what to do with.

"As far as I can tell based on the phone call," Aldo was saying, "you've inherited a patch of land."

Matteo straightened, his attention sharpened. Land.

"She left me property? That could be worth something."

"It appears so," Aldo answered. "Like I said, I don't have a lot of the details just yet. We shouldn't get ahead of ourselves."

Matteo clamped down on the frizzle of excitement now traveling up his spine. Aldo was right. For all he knew, the phone call might have been referring to nothing more than a parking spot.

"Also, there's just a slight caveat."

Matteo pinched the bridge of his nose and resisted the urge to curse out loud. Of course there was. Even this small crumb the universe was throwing his way had to be too good to be true. The way his luck was going so far, he wouldn't expect anything less.

"What's that?"

"Turns out you'll only be getting a part of the property. The other, more substantial part houses a small bed-and-breakfast establishment. The hotel and the land it sits on have been bequeathed to someone else."

Matteo inhaled, his mind quickly processing the information. A bed-and-breakfast sat on part of the property. So it was definitely larger than a parking spot or something similar. All right, he might be able to work with that.

"Who?" Matteo asked. Another long-lost relative perhaps? What were the chances there'd been more than one out there that he hadn't known about?

"I don't have that information yet. Perhaps when the paperwork finally arrives we'll get more details."

Right. Nothing to do but wait. Matteo had somehow found himself in yet another holding pattern.

"Contact me as soon as the documents arrive," he instructed the lawyer. The other man agreed, then ended the call.

Matteo refocused his gaze on the horizon, staring at the distance in the direction where Sardinia, the island in question, would be located. The amount he knew about Sardinia could fit into a thumbnail. He wracked his brain to summon any kind of memory about his long-ago visits but nothing came to mind.

Still, he'd just been presented with a parachute, one that might set him on a direction toward some kind of recovery. One he would have to diligently pursue.

After all, what choice did he have?

Mariana Renati took another large sip of her double espresso and savored the rich, chicory taste. The caffeine was much needed this morning. Not that such wasn't the case most days, but today in particular she needed all the energy she could summon.

He was due to arrive later this morning.

The elusive long-lost son of a long-lost cousin. The man she'd been trying to get a hold of for the past month and a half on Anna's behalf. Only to have her emails go unanswered until it was too late.

The old woman had simply wanted to connect one last time with someone she could call family.

Sure, he'd been apologetic at the end when he'd finally answered her messages. Had told her of his sad, sorry excuse of being busy at work with changes to the family business. Yada yada.

She could guess the truth. Whoever Matteo Talarico was, he had no interest in connecting with a distant elderly relative until he'd heard about what was in it for him.

"Mari, are you back here?"

Roberta's voice sounded from the front of the storage room. She'd been found. Was a few minutes of peace while drinking her morning cup too much to ask for? Today of all days?

She clamped down on her frustration. Rather unreasonable of her to be frustrated at one of her trusty and loyal employees.

That thought gave her a moment of pause. To think. She actually had employees. Roberta and her twenty-something son, Miyko, were in charge of the front office and check-ins/checkouts. Three other born-and-bred Sardinians rounded out the janitorial and cleaning crew. A revolving group of part-time employees made up mostly of college students or bored adults rounded out the staff. It wasn't as if Mari had had anything to do with their hiring. Roberta and Miyko had been a fixture here since Mari had arrived on the island four years ago. The others had mostly been hired alongside her when she'd been brought aboard. Anna's years-long volunteer association with the local university procured the part-time student help.

Still, they all reported directly to her. A fact that had her occasionally riddled with anxiety and self-doubt at the responsibility on her shoulders. Last night she'd woken up no less than three times with her heart racing and covered in perspiration. Twelve people depended on her for their very livelihood now. She'd never felt such a weight on her shoulders.

Which was why this upcoming meeting with this Matteo Talarico was so vitally important. Now that it was finally happening.

But first, she had to go see what Roberta needed.

"*Scusa*, Mari," Roberta began when she reached her side. "The guest from last night, he is asking assistance with the bikes."

Mari could easily guess which guest she was referring to. The man was a regular who checked in every June and always overstayed his welcome. He was from the mainland, with some kind of familial tie to the island. Honestly, Mari couldn't guess why he made the yearly trip or stayed so long. He seemed to be utterly miserable every time he was here.

With a resigned sigh, Mari set her cup down and rose from her lounger chair. She'd done a routine check of all the bikes yesterday evening before wrapping up her nightly chores and retiring sometime after midnight.

"He insists you be the one to help him," Roberta added.

That checked out. The man had also insisted yesterday that she check the espresso machine as something seemed "off" to his apparently highly discerning taste buds. Never mind that her barista was an expert at handling the machine and making a top-notch beverage.

"I'll be right there," Mari answered and took a final swig from her mug. When she arrived at the portico attached to the hotel where they stored the bikes, she found Signore Gio standing hands on hips, a glaring scowl on his face.

"There you are," he said when he saw her approach.

"*Buena sera*, Signore Gio," Mari answered with as wide a smile as she could muster. It wasn't easy. "What seems to be the issue?"

He pointed to the bikes. "These chains all need to be oiled. They're unacceptably dry. How am I supposed to take any of these to ride on the path in the condition they're in? Not a single one is rideable at the moment."

Mari knew without a doubt they weren't that dry. She oiled them weekly. Every Monday, in fact, the day there was the least demand for bikes. Oiling them more often than that would be completely unnecessary. But Signore Gio simply didn't seem to feel complete when he didn't have something to complain about.

Of course, Mari wasn't going to bother explaining any of that to the man. No, she wasn't about to give him what he wanted—an argument. Or a chance to berate her intelligence or competence, as he was wont to do.

Little did Signore Gio know, she had plenty of experience with such scenarios. And people like him. No, strike that. She'd in fact dealt with much worse.

Instead, she increased the wattage of her smile and gave him a friendly nod. "I'll get on it right away, Signore Gio. Which bike would you prefer? I can start with that one."

He looked ready to argue before he gave a dismissive wave of his hand. "It hardly matters. I'm already delayed for the morning. Just get them oiled already and I'll come back after having a cup of coffee."

"Of course," Mari said, fake smile still in place. Poor Esmerelda, she was on espresso and beverage duty this morning. She would have to deal with the ornery old goat for the next few minutes at least.

Mari was oiling the chain on the last bike when she heard footsteps behind her. She sucked in a deep breath as she finished, steeling herself for the second unpleasant encounter of the morning with Signore Gio.

"Ah, you're back. Choose any bike you like," she said, rising and admiring her work as she wiped her hands on a white rag. A smear of black grease marred the terry towel surface.

But when she turned around, forcing yet another fake smile, the man standing before her was most certainly not Signore Gio.

No, the man who'd just walked up behind her didn't resemble Signore Gio in any way. First of all, he had to be at least two decades younger. Tall, imposing, with dark hair and eyes the color of the Sardinian horizon late at night above the cliffs, he looked like he might have stepped out of a cologne ad in an international magazine or embarked from a yacht. For all she knew, he just might have.

Actually, upon further consideration, the two men did indeed have one thing in common. A very displeased expression directed her way. Her current visitor looked about as disgruntled as her previous one had been. Though this one seemed to wear the scowl better.

Mari knew why Signore Gio was upset. But what was up with this guy?

Despite his displeased expression, it was hard to ignore the absolute magnetism of the stranger. Tall, dark and most definitely handsome, the man was the type who no doubt made women swoon.

Not her, however. She had no use for a handsome face. Not anymore.

"I'm looking for a Signora Mariana Renati," he announced, not bothering to introduce himself. "I asked the lady out in the garden, but she brushed me off. Rather rudely, I might add."

He had to be referring to Roberta. She was the only one who might be tending to the flowers at this time of day. And she did tend to get rather frustrated and impatient with any interruption during her gardening time. As if there weren't close to a million other details around the hotel that needed attention. But it was hard to deny Roberta the pleasure she received in tending to the flowers. Still, it wasn't acceptable to be less than hospitable to any of their guests.

"Apologies. I'll be sure to speak to her."

He gave her a dismissive wave of his hand. "Right. So this Mariana person, where might she be?"

"Actually, you've found her." Mari reached her hand out and then snapped it right back upon seeing that the towel hadn't eradicated all the black goo from her skin. "That's me. I'm Mariana."

But who in the world was he? Unless… It couldn't be. Matteo Talarico wasn't due to arrive until much later this afternoon!

He lifted a dark eyebrow. "Do you and your mother have the same name or something?"

What the devil was he talking about? "Uh… no. Can I help you with something, Signore…?"

He ignored her question, his eyes narrowing on her. She'd never seen a man look so handsome while looking so displeased. There probably wasn't much that could make this particular man look anything less, Mari figured.

She gave herself a mental thwack. Enough already. She had to stop lingering on how attractive he was.

"Do you mean to tell me that you're *the* Mariana Renati? The only one?"

Honestly. What was there to be so confused about? "The only one around here. Now, what can I do for you?"

The scowl on his lips transformed into a crooked smirk. Then turned into some semblance of a smile, though it held zero humor.

"Oh, I get it," he said, crossing his arms on his chest in front of the well-tailored shirt he wore.

"Get what?"

"You can't possibly have much experience running a food cart, let alone a hotel. You look like you're barely out of school."

What in the world? "I'm not sure how my age is any of your business." At this point, given his attitude, Mari was past caring who he was. Even if it meant losing a potential future guest. The man was beyond rude. Bordering on boorish. No guest was worth that. Not after what she'd already endured. "You haven't even told me who you are."

"Matteo Talarico."

Mari couldn't suppress her gasp. Well, wasn't this a fine state of affairs. Now that he was finally here, Mari would just as soon ask him to leave. To think, she'd been harping on how good-looking he was just a moment ago. The words he was throwing at her were far less than pretty.

Had she somehow offended this man in the past and forgotten? That didn't seem likely. Matteo Talarico wasn't the kind of man a woman forgot.

"Honestly, is there like some kind of underground club or something? Do you lot meet regularly and discuss individual strategies?" he continued, making no sense whatsoever.

What in the world was he getting at? Did he mean business strategies? If so, she could hardly see why such a thing might bother him so much.

"I honestly have no idea what you're talking about. Nor why you're being quite so rude. Mind if I ask why?"

The smirk widened and he shook his head. "I have a question for you first."

Mari took a deep breath, tried to summon some patience. Fine. She would bite. If only to get to the bottom of all this. "Go ahead," she said, gesturing with her palm up. "Ask away.

And if you're still wondering about my experience, I grew up working in a restaurant. Then went to school for hospitality and spent a couple of years in the field before I got to Sardinia. I've worked here about four years. About half of that time as manager."

Not that she owed this man any kind of explanation. So why was she compelled to be giving him one?

"It appears you're not doing a very good job."

"Of all the—"

"Between the rude employee who greeted me. Then there's the guest in the lobby currently complaining about your watered-down espresso and the lack of adequate bikes."

He actually cut her off! Mari's jaw fell. Granted, those weren't the ideal first impressions she would have had greeting him. Still, he was being unreasonable and jumping to all sorts of conclusions about her competence. "Would you like me to explain any of that to you?" she asked, though she had a hunch what his answer was going to be.

He shook his head. "No. I had another question in mind. How exactly did you manage to bamboozle my mother's cousin into handing the hotel over to you?"

Mari felt the blood drain from her face as his words hit their mark. *How dare he!*

Several beats passed where she could do nothing but stare at his face, his baseless accusation hanging heavy in the air. The breath seemed to have left her lungs. Someone else accusing her of duplicity. Honestly, what was it about her that made men think she could be pushed around with baseless allegations? Did she give off some kind of invisible aura? Was there a hidden sign about her that read "Kick me, I won't fight back"?

No! Not anymore. She vowed long ago that she wouldn't put up with it. This Matteo Talarico had no right to stride in here in his fancy tailored shirt, his shiny polished shoes and killer good looks to try to test that vow after all this time.

Lifting her chin, she breathed deeply through her nose. "I have no idea what you're talking about. Anna asked me months ago when she first fell ill to contact you. Which I did. Repeatedly. You never bothered to respond until she was gone."

That comment seemed to hit the mark. A muscle twitched ever so slightly along his jaw. "She wanted you to have the land adjacent to the hotel. Said that you were a successful businessman who would know how to put it to use."

"Yet she gave the hotel itself to you. An inexperienced novice who worked for her for less than five years. Doesn't that sound the slightest bit 'off' to you?"

That settled it. She'd had more than enough. "I think you should leave, Mr. Talarico."

"We have things we need to discuss."

"We can discuss them through our solicitors. Goodbye."

He appeared ready to argue. Mari held her breath for the length of time it took him to finally dip his head in a nod.

"Fine. I'll go. For now," he added before she could take a breath of relief.

"By the way," he tossed over his shoulder as he turned away toward the door. "You have a dark smudge on your face. Right cheek."

CHAPTER TWO

HE SHOULD HAVE done this first.

Instead of making a beeline straight to the hotel to go and find her, he should have taken the time to do exactly what he was doing now. Taking just a few minutes to gather his thoughts. And getting some rest after a busy travel morning. But he'd blown it.

What had gotten into him? He never operated on emotion.

Not that it was any kind of excuse, but the combination of jet lag, utter disappointment at his father's recklessness and the crushing weight on his shoulders to keep some small part of Tala Industries afloat, the small number of staff who still depended on him for their livelihood. It had all brewed together into a raging storm within his core. So he'd taken it out on the one person on the planet who might be able to help him with what he hoped to accomplish.

What an awful first impression.

If he was being completely honest with himself, he'd have to admit that laying eyes upon Mariana Renati had come as a bit of a surprise. That certainly hadn't helped to temper the way he'd reacted to her. He hadn't been expecting someone quite so...*striking*. It was the first word that came to mind. Even grimy with a smudge of grease on her cheek, Matteo had been struck by the extraordinary hue of her eyes, the way her hair fell in loose tendrils around her rosy cheeks. How lush and red her full lips were.

Upon finding out she was *the* Mariana Renati, the inheritor of the hotel, his suspicions had simply taken over. Still, he should have reined in his reaction.

If only he had come here first. The beachside ristorante slash bar he was seated at offered a perfect view of the crystal-blue water of Poetto Beach. Framed on one side by the looming cliff known as the Sella del Diavolo, the Devil's Saddle, the scene could have been lifted from a Renaissance painting. Matteo vaguely recalled the legend behind the name. Something about a biblical battle where the devil himself was knocked off his demon steed and dropped his saddle onto the side of a mountain, breaking a bite-shaped chunk off the cliffside. If anyone were to ask him, the landmark looked more like a large piece of brownie with a bite taken off the top. The Devil's Bite Mark might have been a more suitable name.

His meandering thoughts were interrupted when the petite waitress in a black miniskirt and crop top placed a sweaty bottle of ale on the table in front of him.

"Grazie," he said, not hesitating to take a long, refreshing gulp. He was already starting to feel less out of sorts. Only, the easing of his ire served to bring about the rising tide of guilt.

He'd really been out of bounds back there with Mariana Renati. Matteo cringed inwardly as he recalled his childish taunt as he was leaving about the smudge of grease on her face. How utterly petty of him. If he had to be further honest with himself, he'd have to admit that part of his frustration had involved the wayward thought that she looked rather cute, unaware of the blemish below her greenish hazel eye and shapely dark eyebrow. Or how much he had to resist the urge to reach over and rub the smudge off her face with his finger.

Well, that was enough of that. Things were complicated enough between him and the pretty manager without adding an inconvenient dose of attraction to the mix.

So he'd taunted her about it instead.

As if his thoughts conjured her, Mari appeared a few feet in front of him on the beach, lugging a large beach umbrella under one arm and the leg of a long lounge chair hoisted on the other shoulder.

That had to take quite a bit of strength.

So she was physically strong as well. It wasn't lost on him that the way she'd stood up to him back there proved no small amount of inner fortitude. She'd actually kicked him out!

Mariana was accompanied by a portly elderly woman in a bright floral swimsuit.

The petite waitress reappeared at the table. "Can I get you another?" she asked, pointing to the nearly empty bottle of ale. He'd been thirstier than he thought.

"Not just yet," he answered, his gaze still focused on Mari as she thrust the sharp end of the large umbrella into the stand. Matteo couldn't help but be impressed. She got the handle in several inches.

"Actually, I was wondering if I should go help with setting up that umbrella," he said.

The waitress followed his gaze and let out a small chuckle. "No need. She'll have it up in no time. That signorina is a pro. Mari does three or four a day for her guests."

Mari. The use of the affectionate nickname wasn't lost on him. It appeared the pretty hotel manager had endeared herself to at least one member of the staff at the eatery across the road from her business.

And he had to accept that the hotel was indeed hers. Though he had every intention of changing that fact first chance he got. If he got his hands on the hotel and the land it sat on, he could begin the process of rebuilding Tala Industries. The building could easily be turned into a condo complex with some renovations, guaranteeing a steady flow of income as soon as the units were ready to rent. The land would serve as collateral for the funds he'd need to start the process. The small patch he'd been granted himself wouldn't be enough to secure any kind of loan. No, he needed all that had been bequeathed to Mari. In return, he would guarantee she was compensated handsomely as soon as he could pay her. Somehow, he was going to have to convince her that his ideas would be a win-win for them both. That was the goal, anyway.

He'd just have to go about it in a better way than barging into her place of business and acting angry and confrontational.

It had just come as such a shock when he'd first laid eyes on her. He wasn't expecting someone like her to be the manager in question. Though he could see how wrong he'd been on that score. Between the way she'd handled him earlier and the way she was competently setting up a spot for her elderly guest on the beach, there was more to the woman than met the eye.

Never judge a book by its cover and all that. He wouldn't make the mistake of underestimating her again. Still, it was rather odd that his mother's cousin had bequeathed the hotel to an employee. Quite the inheritance for someone who wasn't blood. Mari may have impressed him, but he would still fully get to the bottom of exactly what she'd done to be granted such an inheritance. So help him, if there'd been any kind of duplicity involved, he would make sure to address it.

He was getting rather tired of those who would cross a Talarico.

Regardless, Matteo would have to at least pretend to be amiable.

"Actually, there isn't much Mari can't do," his server added with no small amount of admiration clear in her voice.

Matteo was beginning to get that distinct impression of Mari Renati himself.

* * *

Try as she might, Mari just couldn't get this morning's fiasco out of her head. Her mind's eye kept replaying the conversation—or rather, the altercation, to be more accurate—with Matteo Talarico like a film loop over and over.

The nerve of that man. She knew the type all too well. Privileged, successful, used to getting his own way. Men like him expected the world to kneel at their feet. Well, she certainly wasn't about to. No one would hold such power over her ever again. A flush of shame washed over her that she'd ever let it happen in the first place.

Her only excuse was that she'd been young and naive when she'd begun dating Trevor. At first, she'd been both surprised and honored that someone like him would even notice her, let alone want to pursue her romantically. His well-heeled family made no secret of the fact that they thought Mari was well beneath someone like their son. It didn't take much for Trevor himself to reach the same conclusion.

She pushed the thoughts away and made herself hop off the trip down memory lane. Matteo Talarico was the one to thank for the ride.

"I don't know why you bother cleaning this pool," Roberta's voice sounded from across the patio as Mari fished yet another black fly out with the long pole netting.

"It's not like anyone ever uses it," she added a moment later. "Not with a world-renowned beach right across the roadway."

Mari bit back the snippy response that formed on her tongue. Roberta was very good at critiquing her, but Mari chose to believe that it came from good intentions. Still, after this morning's unpleasantness, she just didn't feel like hearing any more about just how inadequate she was.

"Be that as it may," she began in as smooth a voice as she could muster, "the pool should be kept clean in case anyone does want to use it."

Roberta's response was a loud "hmph."

"Shouldn't you be at the desk?" Mari inquired. It was past noon and typically the time their guests began to trickle in. "Miyko should be preparing for the afternoon's aperitif with the chef."

"I'm getting there," Roberta answered with a dismissive wave of her hand. "Though I'm not sure why you're wasting time out here. You could be tending to the guests yourself."

And what exactly would that leave Roberta to do? She was thinking of a tactful way to ask that question when a rich, deep voice sounded from the screen door that led to the hotel foyer.

"Sorry to interrupt, but there was no one at the desk."

She'd only heard it once before but there was no mistaking it. *He* was back. A strange and unfamiliar shiver ran down the length of Mari's spine.

Honestly. What was it with her physical reaction to the man?

It was bad enough he'd shown up earlier when Signore Gio was complaining; now he'd caught them with an unattended front desk.

Mari caught the netting pole just in time before it dropped out of her hand and fell into the pool. As disoriented as he was, she might very well have followed it into the water. That would have been just the icing on the cake. First she argues with him with bicycle grease smeared on her face and then gives him the pleasure of watching her fall into a pool fully clothed.

Thank the deities above she hadn't given him that satisfaction.

She didn't bother to look in his direction. "I'm afraid we're all booked, Signore Talarico. You will have to find other lodgings."

She glanced up just long enough to see him

thrust his hands in his pockets. She didn't dare look at his face. No doubt he was glaring at her. What did he want anyway? Was he here to chide her some more?

"We're booked?" Roberta piped up. "News to me. I thought that Swedish family canceled just this morning."

Damn it, Roberta. For once could she have picked up on a cue?

"I think it's more that I'm not welcome here," he answered the other woman.

"Why? What'd you do?" Roberta wanted to know.

Mari gripped the pole in her hand tight enough that her knuckles turned white. Looked like she wasn't going to be able to ignore Signore Talarico's second unwanted visit of the day. And it was unwanted, wasn't it?

What a silly thought. Of course it was.

Setting the netting down, she swiped her hands down her shorts, resisting the urge to wipe her face in case she hadn't gotten all the grease off. She had, hadn't she?

Enough with the self-questioning already.

"Roberta, please go tend to the desk, as I'm sure we'll have guests arriving. I'd hate for them to be greeted by an empty chair, just like Signore Talarico here."

Roberta stood there a moment longer, her gaze shifting from one of them to the other. If Mari didn't know better, she might have said the older woman appeared amused. Finally, she threw up her hands and made her way to the pathway that led to the front door of the hotel.

Mari glared at Matteo from across the pool as soon as Roberta's shadow cleared the gate. "I believe I was very clear that any further communication between us would need to go through third-party channels."

He bounced once on his polished heels. "Look, for what it's worth, I'm back here to apologize. I was incredibly rude earlier. And you had every right to make me leave."

Huh. She hadn't seen that coming. He didn't seem the type to apologize often. This had to be some kind of act.

"I am genuinely sorry for my behavior."

Mari crossed her arms in front of her chest, not ready just yet to accept his remorse. For all she knew, his words weren't even sincere. Maybe he was just embarrassed.

Still, she was begrudgingly tempted to welcome his apology as he gazed at her with those dark eyes and sensually set mouth.

"You would have every right to ask me to leave again. But I'd really wish you would hear me out. We have a lot to talk about. Do you know how long it takes to have an attorney draft even the simplest note and how much they bill for it?"

"Some things are worth the money. Avoiding you certainly would be worth any amount."

He grimaced and clasped a hand to his chest. "Ouch. I suppose I deserved that."

"You absolutely did. For the record, what exactly were you accusing me of?"

He shook his head. "I was wrong to accuse you of anything. Mea culpa."

Mari felt a softening around the hardness in her chest. She wanted to curse herself for it. It shouldn't be that easy for him to douse the flame of her ire so quickly. No doubt that charming smile of his and those smoldering good looks proved quite effective at soothing feminine anger. Well, she wasn't about to let it work on her.

"Fine," she bit out. "You've said your apology. Now if there's nothing else for the moment, I have things to do."

He didn't get the hint. Just stood staring at her as if studying an unfamiliar object he couldn't quite discern.

Well, that made them somewhat even. She wasn't quite sure what to make of him either.

Except to note that her heart was pounding in her chest and her cheeks felt flushed.

And it had nothing to do with the late June heat.

She was a hard worker. He had to give her that. In fact, it appeared like she was the only one who did do any kind of work around here. Maybe that quality of hers was what drove his relative to bequeath her with such a large inheritance. But plenty of people throughout the world worked hard without being granted an established hotel for their efforts, for heaven's sake. The old woman could have simply gifted her with a sum of money and a guarantee that she could continue her employment.

"You have to admit," he began, though she wasn't even looking at him any longer, "it's a strange way to distribute her assets. The established hotel to an employee. The smaller plot of land adjacent she gives to blood kin. You can't blame me for being somewhat curious."

She stopped her chore to send an intense glare his way. "Is that how you were behaving earlier today, then? Curiously?"

"Look, I said I was sorry. It just took me by surprise. Usually, assets as grand as hotels are left to family members."

The intensity of the glare grew. As did the reddish hue coloring her cheeks. The strain of her chore had her skin glistening in the sun with a sheen of sweat. Her hair was a mess of curls atop her head, a few tendrils escaping out of the tight knot to wisp about her shoulders. Under any other circumstances—say, if they'd run into each other at a function or in any piazza—he might have asked her out. She was certainly attractive, curvy in all the right places, lush lips perfect for kissing.

And that was quite enough of that. He had absolutely no business appreciating how kissable her mouth appeared. So not what he was here for.

The woman found him disdainful, for heaven's sake. As made evident by her next words. "I don't suppose that it might have ever occurred to you that Anna might have considered me as family?"

Well, when she put it that way. "You know what I mean. Typically, blood ties trump all others."

She nodded once. "Right. I think I might know what blood ties you might be referring to. Like blood relatives who pay no attention to notices alerting them that their family member is ill? Who don't respond right away or make any kind of effort to come be by their relative's side before the end? To hold their hand and offer words of comfort and love."

She had him there. If he had to guess, Matteo would say that Mari had done all the above and more.

"You speak the truth, of course. I should have made more of an effort to respond to your messages and find out what was going on with Anna. It's been something of a tough year and I've been dealing with a lot." Like the loss of a generation's worth of corporate development, not to mention name recognition. Thanks to his father.

Mari didn't seem impressed with his excuse. If looks could kill, he might have been dead and buried by now. She began to gradually pull the long pole out of the pool and carried it to a shed behind her. Matteo got the distinct feeling he'd just been silently dismissed.

Ha! She wasn't going to get rid of him that easy. Several moments passed while she remained in the shed. He was beginning to wonder if she was going to try and wait him out. That would leave him with very few options. He couldn't very well corner her in there. That would be downright creepy.

And he certainly wasn't about to partake in a game of "come out, come out, little pretty."

A sigh of relief escaped his lips when she finally reappeared out of the shadows of the small space.

"You're still here," she declared.

He'd never met a woman who managed to charm him while being downright annoyed with his mere presence. Maybe it was the cute crop bathing suit top she had on over loose-fitting gym shorts. Maybe it was the way her tanned skin had him imagining how it might feel to the touch.

Matteo swallowed a curse. There he went again.

What was wrong with him? The answer was obvious. He'd been without female companionship for too long. When was the last time he'd been on a date? The fiasco with Tala Industries had taken up all his time and energy for the past several months. All for naught. Had to have been way too long ago, by the look of things. Otherwise, he wouldn't be thinking of this woman in anything but an adversarial way, especially considering how angry she was with him still. His apology had done zero good, it appeared.

"Will you leave if I were to say I accept your apology?" she asked.

"It would certainly help to make me feel better. Though I doubt you'd be saying so with any kind of sincerity."

"Lies can be sincere," she answered with a small smile.

Matteo honestly had no idea how to respond to that. "Don't you think we need to have at least some sort of conversation about all this? I'll be the owner of the land right adjacent to this hotel that you happen to own."

Land that was absolutely useless to him unless he could get this woman to agree to give up ownership of what she'd been bequeathed.

"Are you saying we'll be neighbors?" she asked, walking around the length of the pool and past him toward the colorful garden between the patio area and the reception lobby.

"At the least. Don't you want to know what ways I'm considering developing that land?"

That was a bluff. There was really nothing to develop the empty space to. Another hotel right next door would be redundant, the strip had plenty of restaurants already and food service wasn't particularly his forte. He needed the building and the land it stood on for collateral. Everything Tala Industries owned was already fully leveraged or liquidated.

No, for what he wanted to do with what he'd been given he would need her full cooperation.

At the moment, she seemed anything but co-operative. He would just have to see what he could do about that.

CHAPTER THREE

As much as she hated to admit it, Matteo Talarico was right. They did need to talk. Mari felt the weight of his presence behind her as she walked out of the patio and made her way to the flower garden that separated the pool deck area from the front lobby.

She'd chosen to come this way on purpose. Being in this space always served to soothe and calm her. The rich colorful flowers, the floral scent that drifted in the air on a soft breeze. The little patch of land between the patio and the building could always be counted on as a small oasis of tranquility. Sometimes, when one of those mid-sleep panic attacks struck, she even came out here in the middle of the night.

Funny, the garden's soothing effect didn't seem to be working quite so well at the moment. Mari's pulse was still racing. She could still feel heat burning in her cheeks. Something about this man had her reacting physically in ways she couldn't explain, nor did she like.

It made absolutely no sense. Yet her body didn't seem to want to listen to reason.

"Wow," he said behind her. She turned around to find him staring at the flower bushes, an expression of marvel on his face. "This place is something else."

All right. That was a point in his favor, albeit granted unwanted. She might not have taken him as the type of man to notice and appreciate a well-tended garden.

"This was Anna's masterpiece. She spent hours and hours out here. Until…until she couldn't. We're trying to keep it intact as best we can. Roberta's taken over its care. She's the older woman you saw in the lobby when you first arrived."

"It's like its own little oasis."

That was a rather charming way to describe it. Charming was also a good way to describe Matteo this time around. The man had the looks of a cologne ad model and despite their first rather tumultuous meeting, she had to admit he was beyond charismatic.

If only he had introduced himself as the prince charming type upon meeting. And therein lay the issue. If she were being honest with herself, she would have to admit that a great part of her ire with Matteo was that his words had hit rather close to their target. Maybe she really did have no business trying to run this place. Had Anna even been in sound mind when she'd asked to change her will to hand the hotel to Mari? What if she hadn't been? What if this place failed after all these years and it was due to her incompetence?

Breathe. Just breathe. Nice and deep.

"I barely remember her," Matteo said, tugging her out of her thoughts. His gaze returned to her face. "I'm surprised she remembered me."

Mari nodded. "She did. Even as her mind started to go toward the end. She spoke of you occasionally. Said you were precocious and curious as a child. Wandered around this place like you owned it."

He flashed her a charming grin. "I still get that from people. A lot."

"Color me shocked," she said, inserting as much sarcasm into the words as she could.

"So, she did all this, huh?" he asked, gesturing around to the bounty of flowers that surrounded them.

"Yes. We have a lawn service for maintenance. But other than that, this was all her doing."

He thrust his hands into his pockets, an action she was beginning to see was rather an ingrained habit for him. His eyes focused on her once more.

"I regret not visiting more. And it's inexcusable that my parents eventually stopped visiting altogether."

He wasn't going to get any kind of argument from her on that score.

"On top of discussing our respective inheritances, I'd love to hear more about her. Please, let me buy you dinner later tonight. Maybe in the piazza?"

The offer took her by surprise. Surely, she wasn't even going to entertain the thought.

Before she could answer, Miyko appeared from around the pathway. Dressed in a colorful romper complete with a bright purple ascot around his neck, he blended quite nicely with the surrounding flowers. His face, however, was anything but cheery. It took a lot to irritate her first assistant, and he was clearly irritated. She didn't have to grasp at straws to guess as to why.

"He's asking for you again," he said, pausing mid-speech to look Matteo up and down before turning back to her. "In the lobby. Refuses to tell me what the issue is. I promise I tried to get it out of him."

Mari rubbed her forehead and cursed inside. Great. Now she would have to contend with Signore Gio again on top of everything else. To make matters worse, Matteo was here to witness it all this time. More proof of her incompetence in the form of a dissatisfied guest.

"I don't suppose you can tell him I'm busy and convince him to let me go find him later?"

Miyko tilted his head and thrust his fists onto his hips. "What do you think? I tried that in the first place."

It was worth a shot, though she'd known the attempt would be futile. "All right, I'll go see what he wants."

As expected, Matteo followed them both down the path to the front lobby, where a rust-faced Signore Gio stood glaring at the doorway.

"What can I help you with this afternoon?" Mari asked, her voice friendly and accommodating. Though a lot of good that would do. There really seemed to be no way to placate the man. She knew the exact day and time he was due to check out. She was counting the minutes. The day couldn't come soon enough. Then she wouldn't even have to think about him again until next year.

But that wasn't the case this morning. Today she was going to have to work to appease Signore Gio yet again. This time with an audience that included the one man she really didn't want witnessing her struggles with a disgruntled guest. He'd already judged her once and found her lacking, apology or not.

Signore Gio crossed his arms in front of his chest. "The temperature in my room is quite uncomfortable. I'd like it much cooler. It's as hot as a Turkish bath in there."

"I see. Did you try lowering the climate adjustment gauge?" She wouldn't put it past the man to skip that logical step before seeking her out simply to harass her.

Signore Gio rolled his eyes so dramatically she wondered if it would give him a headache. "Honestly. Of course I did. What kind of dolt do you take me for?"

Mari figured he really didn't want her to answer that question. "I had to ask."

The man shook his head slowly with lips pursed. "No, no you really didn't."

Mari resisted the urge to glance in Matteo's direction. He probably found her getting tongue-lashed by Signore Gio quite entertaining.

"Why don't you give me a chance to change and I'll run up and take a look at it myself."

"It's the least you can do," Gio said. "And I'd prefer if you came up right away. Rude of you to ask me to wait."

Rude? He had just called *her* rude? Of all the hypocritical…

Mari mustered all her patience and took a deep breath before speaking. "I understand you're unhappy with the temperature in your room, Signore Gio. We will make sure it gets resolved. If I can't figure it out, I'll have an order sent to the maintenance service right away. But first, I'm going to go at least throw a T-shirt on. It will only take a moment."

"No."

The simple word took her aback. *No.* Even for Signore Gio it seemed rather harsh. Cruel even.

No acknowledgment or consideration of her request whatsoever. As if her thoughts or feelings on the matter meant absolutely nothing. As if she herself meant nothing. Like it was okay to treat her as insignificant, a mere cog in the machine to be ordered around according to his whims.

Treating her just as too many others had in the past.

At least with Signore Gio, it wasn't personal. Except that it was. It would always be personal. How could it not be?

Mari spent several moments trying to figure out what to say. Words seemed to escape her. And then she felt a gentle touch on her elbow from behind. So slight, she might have imagined it. But then she felt his heat behind her and she knew it was real. Matteo.

If she didn't know better, she might guess that he was touching her as a show of support. Boosting her confidence. That was unexpected.

But darned if it didn't work.

Matteo standing behind her gave her just the nudge she needed to snap out of her shock and stupor. Inhaling deeply, she straightened her spine and lifted her chin.

She chose her words carefully, apologizing politely. *"Mi dispiace,"* she began in Italian. "The thermostat issue hardly constitutes an immediate emergency. I will be up to your room as soon as I've thrown a shirt on, signore."

She locked eyes with the older gentleman and didn't so much as blink.

After several beats passed, Signore Gio appeared ready to argue. Mari preempted him with a cross of her arms over her chest. She was done fighting but she would stand her ground. It would just take some more practice. And Signore Gio was certainly giving her plenty of opportunities to practice.

The older man's lips tightened and his skin flushed a deep pink. Mari half expected him to stomp his feet. Finally, he pivoted on his heel and turned to walk back to the hotel. "Do not take more than five minutes," he demanded as he walked away.

Mari finally released the breath she'd been holding and allowed her shoulders to droop in relaxation. Though she'd have to deal with him again in a few short minutes, at least this was one small battle won.

For now.

Plus, she had a more immediate concern. Matteo remained standing behind her, touching her still. The gentlest of touches, just at the base of her elbow. Yet it was enough to send currents of electricity through her arm and up her spine.

What was that about? Why was she physically reacting to his touch? Whatever the reason, it wasn't a good one.

She stepped away and turned to face him.

He began a slow clap. "Bravo. That was handled beautifully."

Silly. But she felt a jolt of pleasure run over her skin at his compliment. "I've had plenty of practice over the years."

He lifted a single eyebrow. "Oh?"

She really shouldn't have said that. "Well, I should get going. Don't want to make Signore Gio any crankier than he already is."

"That's a pretty low bar," Matteo said, turning to stare in the direction Signore Gio had just walked.

"Don't I know it."

"Would you like company when you go to his room? I could come with you."

The offer took her by surprise. Hard to believe this was the same man who'd stormed into the portico this morning to accuse her of swindling a little old lady. This newer version of Matteo Talarico was throwing her off in all manner of ways. As tempted as she was to take him up on his generosity, she really didn't want to face Signore Gio by herself, especially if his thermostat issue wasn't going to be an easy fix.

But she was the manager here. Actually, as of a few months ago, she was even more than that. She was now the owner of the establishment. How would it look if she couldn't handle a simple maintenance request without an emotional support buddy by her side?

"Thank you, but that won't be necessary," she answered. "I'm a big girl. I can handle it myself." She gave him a small smile before turning toward the stairway.

"I have no doubt," Mari heard him say as she walked away.

At least one of them was sure.

* * *

"Well, that didn't take terribly long."

Matteo was still in the lobby when Mari made her way back downstairs from Signore Gio's room. Her stomach made an unexpected little flip upon seeing him. Yet another unwelcome physical reaction to him. No denying that it was anything but excitement. Which made no sense at all. She wanted to be rid of the man, for heaven's sake.

"That's because Signore Gio was adjusting the thermostat for the hot-tub on his patio and not the temperature-control dial for his room."

"Huh. Did he have the decency to apologize for his mistake?"

Mari couldn't contain her chuckle. "On the contrary. He said we shouldn't have dials for each that look so similar. Or that we should have marked them more clearly. Never mind that there's a clear picture of a hot tub above one of them."

"I see. You have your hands full with that one." He bounced on his heel. "So you never answered me," he said a moment later.

"I'm sorry, I seem to have forgotten the question."

"I asked if you'd let me take you to dinner."

As he said the last word, Mari's traitorous stomach made a grumbling sound so loud she wondered if the beachgoers beyond the path might have heard it. If Matteo heard, which he must have, he was polite enough not to mention it.

"I usually just ask chef to prepare me a tray that I take up to my room."

He tilted his head. "Well, as exciting as that sounds, would you at least consider dining with me instead? We could head to the piazza."

Exciting. He had no idea just how overrated Mari found the notion of excitement. How hard she'd worked to achieve the kind of life that let her relax for a couple of hours in the evening before bed with a quiet dinner and a good book.

No. She'd had quite enough excitement in her previous life.

"Why?" she asked.

"Why should you come to dinner with me?"

She shook her head. "Why are you asking me to?"

His lips settled into a small smile. "Well, partly because there's a lot we need to talk about."

"What's the other part?"

"To give me a chance to at least partially make up for the way I behaved this morning. It's the very least I can do."

That was true enough. Mari surprised herself upon realizing she was actually considering taking him up on his offer. She hadn't been to the piazza in ages. It was a glorious evening, a perfect night to enjoy a meal under the stars in one of the many open-air trattorias the center offered.

So many reasons to say yes. One very big reason to say no. She could fall so easily for the charms of this man. A complication she didn't need in her life at the moment, if ever. Considering how much time they were sure to have to spend together in the coming weeks until this whole estate thing was settled, saying no to him right now was the most sensible path.

Though she really had worked up an appetite dealing with Signore Gio. And chef was preparing Milanese tonight for dinner, a dish she wasn't particularly fond of.

To his credit, Matteo stood waiting patiently for a response. Not a hint of frustration that she was taking too long to answer.

"It's just one dinner," Matteo finally nudged, his smile still slight and friendly. He glanced at his watch. "My flight to Rome doesn't leave for another five hours. You'd be doing me a favor not letting me spend the time meandering the streets of Cagliari by myself and eating solo."

A hint of something shifted in her chest, something she refused to acknowledge as disappointment. "You're flying back tonight?"

He nodded. "Only because I didn't plan very well. Most of the rooms on the island were booked. And the hotel I usually stay in in Rome has a suite on standby for me."

Right. Matteo Talarico was the type of man luxury hotels reserved suites for. In other words, he was completely out of her league. Which was a ridiculous thought anyway. After all, he was attempting to apologize to her. The last man she'd been involved with was completely unfamiliar with the concept. Trevor was much more talented in the art of gaslighting her into believing that everything that went wrong was her fault. Silly of her to even compare the two men, really.

"So what do you say?" Matteo asked again.

As if to completely mock her once again, another low grumble echoed from the vicinity of her stomach.

This time, Matteo didn't hide his amusement. He released a low chuckle and winked at her. The wink was what finally did it. The last of her resistance seemed to crumble like a collapsing wall.

"All right. But only because I've worked up an appetite."

He clasped a hand to his chest in exaggerated horror. "You wound me. I thought it was my charm that finally convinced you and not your hunger pangs."

She begrudgingly returned his laugh. "Actually, there's another reason."

That head tilt again, as if he couldn't quite figure her out. Well, she could say the same of him.

"What's that?" he asked.

"For Anna. You aunt must have had some kind of faith in you that led her to bequeathing you part of her estate. Despite not having set eyes on you as an adult."

Mari had a lot to thank Anna for. The least she could do was give her partial heir a few minutes to hear him out.

She could only hope she wouldn't regret it.

CHAPTER FOUR

MATTEO FELT AN unreasonable amount of relief when she finally agreed to his offer of dinner.

"I'll just be a minute. Let me freshen up a bit and grab my bag."

"Sure thing," he answered, walking over to the small love seat at the center of the lobby and sitting down. "Guess I'll just loiter in your lobby a little longer."

Mari studied him up and down, as if sizing him up. Again.

She tapped her chin, as if coming to a conclusion. "We can't have our guests thinking we have a loiterer. Even one as well dressed as you are."

"I imagine that wouldn't look good."

She nodded. "It wouldn't. What if they jump to the wrong conclusion that we weren't prepared for a reservation and had you waiting all this time for a room?"

"Good point." The way she was always thinking about her responsibility to this place kept impressing him. For someone so relatively young with limited experience, she fit the role well.

Well, that was neither here nor there. He still had a goal here. He'd be willing to compromise, even offer her the opportunity to stay in her current roll. Win-win all around. But the end game couldn't change. He needed her to relinquish her part of this estate.

"Why don't you come down with me? I won't take long to get ready. Just going to brush my hair out and freshen up a bit."

"All right," Matteo answered, wondering if the moment implied some kind of marker between them, a development of some kind of trust. She led him past the check-in desk, through a small office that housed two wooden desks that faced each other and past a narrow hallway to a steel door that opened up to a narrow stairway that led down. They were descending to the deepest caverns of the Hotel Nautica.

Finally, they reached a door with a number panel lock. Mari quickly entered a combination and the door swung open to the inside. He followed her into a small apartment furnished with two love seats that faced a colorful hanging tapestry on the opposite wall. A small kitchenette to the side divided the living space. No television. No end tables. Yet the apartment still exuded a sense of coziness and comfort.

"I'll just be a minute," Mari repeated and walked through a doorway Matteo assumed had to lead to her bedroom. Surprising, really. She could have her pick of living quarters in this hotel. From what he'd seen online, some of the suites were downright ritzy with ample space and personal patios sporting luxurious hot-tubs. Yet she'd chosen to live in a small, unassuming apartment deep in the basement.

He studied the space while he waited. She'd certainly made the best of the limited area. The walls were painted a cheery light green, and a three-tier shelf against the opposite wall housed several potted plants. A postage-stamp-sized window sat high on the wall bordering the ceiling and offered a surprising amount of natural light for this time of day.

More than what he did see, Matteo was struck by what was missing. Not that he was looking for clues, but there was nothing here that offered any kind of information about who Mariana Renati truly was. The only photographs on the walls were pictures of various famous landmarks around Cagliari, including the Devil's Saddle cliff. A couple of grand churches. He strode over to a smaller framed photo by the plant shelf, the only photo that featured any people in it. Mari stood in the center smiling between an older woman and the man who manned the desk downstairs. The woman had eyes the same shade as his own. She had to be Anna, his mother's distant cousin. They stood in the garden of the hotel.

Nothing in here gave him any kind of idea about where Mari came from. How she found her way to Sardinia, of all places. He had no doubt she was American; the accent was unmistakable. If he had to guess, he would say she'd made her home in New England a good number of years. Not that he could tell from anything in here. Like she didn't exist until she arrived in Sardinia.

Matteo gave himself a mental shake. Honestly, why did it matter? He didn't need to know anything about Mari Renati aside from what it would take to convince her to turn over her share of this property to him.

He didn't need to know her life story, for Pete's sake. There was no reason for him to be so curious about her.

He heard her bedroom door open behind him, then turned to find Mari already ready to leave.

"That was fast."

She shrugged. "I am rather hungry. And I figured you didn't want to be kept waiting."

Matteo took a moment to study her. She'd unclipped her hair and it now hung in soft, thick waves over her shoulders. A bright red sundress showed off the bronze tan of her skin. She'd added a dab of color to her lips but as far as he could tell she wore no makeup.

Fetching.

The untoward thought echoed through his head without warning. But there was no denying that Mari was a very attractive woman. He'd dated far more glamorous women, women who spent an inordinate of time and mass amounts of money prepping for the simplest of outings. Mari had taken less than ten minutes and he was downright struck by how attractive she looked in a simple red dress and open-toe sandals. Toes that were painted a neon blue color that matched a stone ankle bracelet she wore above her left foot.

That settled it. He must be hungry too. Or perhaps jet-lagged still. Clearly, he wasn't thinking straight. When had he ever noticed a woman's toes before?

"Matteo?" she asked, a curious smile on her lips. "Did you want to get going?"

Great. He'd been caught practically gawking at her.

"More than ready. Let's go," he said, extending his arm in a gesture to have her lead the way.

A moment later, they were on the sidewalk in front of the hotel. He followed her onto the paved pathway between the steel gate and the beach.

The businessman in Matteo immediately made several more observations on top of the ones he'd already noted. This really was the ideal place for an establishment such as the one he had in mind. On a busy public path and crowded beach. The location offered the perfect opportunity for anyone looking for an ideal relaxing Italian residence. With Rome a fast plane ride away, a person could be certain to enjoy the best of what Italy had to offer. Island sights and beaches and the sightseeing opportunities of one of its major cities. It was a wonder Tala hadn't ventured to this part of Italy already. His mind reeled with the possibilities running through his head, all the ways a luxurious condo building would thrive in such a place. But first he had to convince Mari to relinquish her ownership.

If only Anna had left the entire property to him solely, he could get started right away. On top of giving him another chance to rebuild what his father had destroyed by bankrupting them, this project could give Matteo a true opportunity to create something from the ground up by himself. A chance to finally prove himself by saving them from the disaster his parent had thrust them all into.

Mari snapped him out his thoughts. He wasn't sure if he'd heard her correctly.

"What was that?" he asked.

"I said, if we walk somewhat quickly, we should catch the coming bus and not have to wait for the next one in twenty minutes."

Bus?

"We're taking public transportation?" he asked, belatedly realizing he'd been blindly following her off the pathway and down the residential street behind the hotel.

She didn't bother pausing, glancing at him sideways. "It's the most economical and most convenient way to get to the piazza."

Matteo didn't bother to try and recall the last time he'd taken a public bus anywhere. The answer was never. The closest he'd ever come was a party bus his friend Gus had rented for his bachelor stag activities in Toronto to take them from casinos to clubs and back to their hotel. So not the same.

"It will take us right to the harbor, and it's a quick walk to the piazza from there."

"I see. Couldn't we just call a car?"

He couldn't interpret the smile she sent his way. "We're almost there. The bus will get here by the time you arrange for a ride. And I don't know about you, but I could use a walk in the fresh sea air."

She paused a moment before asking, "You do walk occasionally, don't you? Or do you mean to tell me you take cars whenever you need to go somewhere."

"Of course I walk." That was true enough. He wasn't going to specify that most of his walking was done as a warm-up preceding a punishing run on the treadmill in a dedicated room of his penthouse apartment full of gym equipment. The fact was, she was right that he typically took a car service whenever he needed to travel within the city. It was simply a matter of efficiency. Interesting that she had him figured out in so many small ways.

A moment later, they were crossing a busy intersection to reach a covered stand smattered with various film posters and advertising flyers. A handful of other people stood waiting, including a young woman gently nudging a stroller back and forth, as well as a harried-looking man in a business suit and messenger bag scrolling frantically on his phone. The Devil's Saddle framed the skyline behind them against the backdrop of crystal-blue sky dotted with puffy white clouds. If he were to pick any day to walk, this wouldn't be a bad one to choose. And he certainly couldn't ask for better company.

The last thought gave him pause. If he were to examine it closely, despite having just met Mari, he was beginning to genuinely enjoy being around her. She was the type of person who seemed to bring a certain joy out into the world surrounding her.

"Let's go," Mari said behind him, taking him by the forearm and tugging him across the street. In his distraction, he hadn't even noticed the neon sign of the stick figure walking on the streetlight. Nor had he noticed that a large bus with wide glass windows was rapidly approaching from the other side. "I don't want to miss it. Most of the drivers are friendly and cordial but some of them can be complete—" The last word was cut off by the noisy brakes of the bus as it came to a stop. Though he could guess the general intent of whatever she'd said.

Matteo dashed behind her, skirting a revving motorcycle who'd stopped too far past the white crossing line. Honestly, he didn't understand her panic. If they did miss the bus, they could in fact go ahead with his preferred option of hailing a cab or calling a car service. But darned if he didn't get a small rush of adrenaline running past Mari to make it to the stop before the bus arrived. As if he were back to being a small boy competing in a lawn race with one of the staffers he'd spent too much time with as a child.

They needn't have worried.

By the time they got there, the young mother was struggling to lift her baby out of the stroller and fold the contraption. The driver dramatically huffed in his seat. The man clearly fell into the latter category Mari had been referring to earlier.

"I'm sorry," the young mother said in a heavy Eastern European accent. "Sometimes the strap gets stuck."

"May I?" Matteo asked her, gesturing to the stroller.

She nodded, stepping back. He didn't bother trying to unclasp the belt the little tyke was secured with, opting instead to lift the entire contraption and carry it up the stairs.

He could have sworn the chubby-cheeked infant smiled at him when he set it down in front of an empty seat and held it securely until Mama arrived.

He looked up to find Mari smiling at him too.

Three stops later, their mode of transportation had grown increasingly crowded. Matteo wasn't about to complain. Mari sat next to him, her arm brushing against his. The flowery scent of her shampoo tickled his nose. It reminded him of the garden they'd been standing in earlier today.

Was that really just this afternoon? He'd felt like he'd lived a month since arriving in Cagliari this morning. And he felt like he'd known the woman next to him much longer than less than a day. Something about Mari evoked a sense of familiarity he couldn't quite explain. He really wished they'd met under different circumstances. Though truth be told, she wasn't the type of woman he would normally expect to find in his orbit. No, his tastes usually ran more cosmopolitan. Definitely not the kind of woman who took a bus into town and cleaned debris out of a pool after sparring with a grumpy old guest at her hotel. The way she'd stood up to the man had been downright impressive. His last romantic relationship had been a short yet heated entanglement involving a French model.

Not that he was thinking of Mari in any kind of romantic way. They were... Well, he couldn't quite say what they were just yet. Fate had thrown them together in a rather unusual way. And right now, she happened to be the one thing standing in his way of obtaining a much-needed goal. He wasn't going to forget that one pertinent fact.

Despite the alluring scent of her hair under his nose.

As if mocking him for the thought, the bus chose that moment to hit a rather significant bump and jostled her up against him. Matteo resisted the strong urge to wrap his arms around her shoulders and hold her there.

She smiled at him awkwardly and shifted back to rest her side against the wall.

"This is our stop," she said a moment later, rising out of her seat.

Matteo followed suit and they exited the bus onto a busy sidewalk. The harbor across the street was dotted with boats both small and large. A massive cruise ship sat docked in the center, dwarfing the other watercraft.

"The plaza will be busy," she informed him as they began a leisurely walk down the street. "Looks like a cruise just came in."

"It never ceases to amaze me how colossal those floating hotels can be built," he said, taking in the sight of what had to be a three-thousand-cabin ship at the least.

"That's exactly what they are," Mari responded as they continued to make their way down the busy and noisy street. "And they need just as much staff to keep the guests happy as the major high-star hotels."

"You sound like you speak from experience."

"I do, as a matter of fact," she answered without elaborating further. There was a story there. One she wasn't willing to tell him. Yet.

They turned the corner and the sidewalk became even more crowded. Loud groups of teenagers entering and exiting cafés, couples holding hands strolling, young and old alike. Families with small children. It appeared the piazza was a draw for all manner of Sardinians this time of day.

"Quite a popular place," he commented, letting her lead the way.

"It typically is this time of year. And this time of day."

It was easy to see why. The center of town seemed to have something to offer everyone. Souvenir shops as well as high-end fashion stores. Fast-food pizzerelli diners as well as fine-dining restaurants with uniformed waiters. And everything in between. Compared with the big cities like Rome and Florence, this seemed more intimate. Cozier.

Maybe flying into Cagliari wouldn't be such a chore after all. He could see himself visiting often once he got the resort established and running.

"I didn't expect it to be quite so...modern," Matteo said, though he wasn't certain he'd reached at the right word. He'd been expecting a small village with a quaint-and-cozy town. Not this bustling and busy community with designer clothing stores and gourmet restaurants.

"Don't be fooled," Mari said. "Cagliari has a lot of history. As does all of Sardinia. These buildings here might be new, but just beyond the center are churches and cathedrals that are centuries old."

Her voice held no small amount of pride. She spoke quite fondly of her adopted homeland. While here he was, planning on setting stakes in this locale with a business he'd be running, and he knew so very little about the island and the town that would house it.

No doubt about it, he was going to need Mari's help to get said business off the ground. So she would have to be a willing participant. He got the feeling that was going to take some work on his end. He would have to give her an incentive to cooperate.

First thing first, he had to establish a rapport between them. Which would hopefully lead to gaining her trust.

And hopefully it wouldn't take long. Matteo had some trusted staff he'd like to move over to the new site and keep gainfully employed without interruption.

Before long, they approached a circular rotary with a tall statue looming in the center. Clearly depicting some kind of regal figure, judging by the crown on its head.

"What an interesting display," Matteo said. "What is that statue supposed to represent? And why is it wearing all that colorful garb?"

Her response was a hearty chuckle. "You really do need a basic lesson on Cagliari's history, don't you?"

"I guess so. What do you suppose we should do about that?"

We. The word hung between them so small yet so powerful. Matteo scrambled for something else to say. How presumptuous of him. As if his lack of knowledge about the island and village were any of her concern.

But perhaps the bigger question was, why was Matteo even thinking about Mariana Renati in such a way, as if they were some kind of team?

Probably because he wanted it to be the truth.

CHAPTER FIVE

We.

Mari really wished he hadn't said what he'd just said. And that he hadn't used that particular word. Only, part of her was maddeningly pleased that he had. Which made zero sense whatsoever. In no way, shape or form would she and Matteo ever be considered any kind of "we." At the most, they would simply be neighbors.

"So, care to start my first lesson, then?" he asked, his gaze still focused on the fifteen-foot-tall statue. "Starting with who this gentleman is exactly?" he added a moment later.

Mari forced herself to return to the topic at hand. It was all too easy to lose her focus when she was around this man. "That's King Carlo Felice," she answered, her gaze following his.

"Huh. And did he like to dress in extravagant colors or something?"

"I'm sure he did. Being a king and all. But the

reason his statue is dressed up is because it's a tribute to our soccer team. The Cagliari Calcio recently won the Serie A cup. The last time that happened was several years ago. I wish I could have been here for all the celebrations. There were fireworks, a grand festival, hundreds of people lined the streets."

He turned away from the statue then to look at her, one eyebrow raised. "You weren't here then?"

She shook her head. "I was still back in the States, hadn't moved to Sardinia yet."

The lone eyebrow remained lifted. "You seem confused?"

He shrugged. "It's just hard to believe that you've been here such a short period of time, given how acclimated you seem to be to the town."

Acclimated. Is that how she sounded? Funny, there were still some days when she felt every bit the outsider here in this part of the world, despite her Italian heritage and devotion to the place.

"How long have you lived here exactly?" Matteo asked.

"About four years, give or take."

"So Anna hired you not long after your arrival."

"Pretty much."

They'd drifted backward away from the statue and close to the traffic circle. A moped cycle blared its horn at them as it passed. Looked like neither one was paying attention to their surroundings. For his part, Matteo appeared genuinely interested in learning more about her. Or how she'd come to be a Sardinian resident, anyway.

Not that she could look too deeply into that. The man was just naturally curious. Or he was simply making conversation. Still, aside from Anna, Mari couldn't recall the last time someone had displayed any kind of interest in her whatsoever.

Except for Trevor, whose betrayal had been sharp and painful. He'd deserted her when she'd needed him the most.

So he knew that much more about Cagliari now. About one of its princes and its football team. An initial lesson in the Italian island's history. As interesting as that was, what he really wanted to know more about was Mari's story. Exactly where had she come from? What had brought her here? Sure, Sardinia was a lovely island, Cagliari a vibrant city with a rich history. But he wanted details about Mari's history.

And why was he so curious about her in the first place?

A curiosity that was maddeningly inconvenient. He wasn't in Sardinia to make friends. Least of all to make a friend of the one woman who was standing in the way of all his plans.

After gazing at the statue a few more minutes, Mari turned to him with a small smile. "Ready to move on?"

Right. They were here for dinner after all.

He held his arm out in front of him. "Lead the way. I am but a devotee in your wake following you where you take me."

"Wow."

"A bit much?"

She nodded, her smile growing wider. "Just a tad. Seeing as I'm merely taking you to grab a bite to eat."

They started walking around the statue past the circular roadway toward a wide hill. "Although," Mari continued, "very few meals in this part of the world would be categorized as a simple bite."

"More so than the mainland?" he asked.

"Oh yes. Italians in general like to linger over their meals. But Sardinians in particular make dinnertime an all-out event."

"Then I say we get started."

They began making their way up the hill past pizzerellis with long lines out front and charming small boutiques. Scattered in between were tourist shops full of small fixtures and colorful magnets in the window.

"I didn't expect it to be quite so…commercial," Matteo said.

"Parts of Cagliari absolutely are," Mari answered, her breath on a slight hitch. The hill was steeper than it had appeared from the square by the statue. Matteo felt a bit out of breath himself, though he was loathe to admit it. "But wait till we get to the top. The gardens and architecture are straight Renaissance Italy."

Before Matteo could reply to that, a sudden blur darted at them from the opposite direction, headed straight for Mari. The helmeted figure showed no signs of slowing down. Her gaze fixated on Matteo, she wasn't going to see him coming.

"Look out!" Matteo barely got the words out as he reached to grab her about the waist and yank her out of the projectile's way. She landed against him, their bodies slammed together. "Skateboarder."

"Uh, thanks," she said, blinking up at him with those sparkling hazel eyes he was growing so familiar with.

It took a second for Matteo to find his own voice. Her scent drifting to his nose, the warmth of her seeping through his clothing. She made no effort to move out of his grasp, and heaven help him, he couldn't seem to loosen his grip on her.

"Scusa!" The kid's voice echoed behind them as he continued barreling down the hill. He didn't sound all that sorry.

"They think it's a thrill to skateboard down the hills," Mari said, her eyes still fixated on his. How had he not noticed before how dark her eyelashes were? Or the way her eyebrows arched so perfectly, just a shade lighter than her hair?

Get a grip.

What in the world was wrong with him? Waxing poetic on a crowded hill about a woman's eyebrows. Maybe that cliché about apples falling from trees might actually apply to him. How easily he was distracted by a pretty face. Just like his old man.

Unacceptable. He made himself release her and managed to step half a foot away.

Mari blinked a couple of more times, then straightened the hemline of her dress. "It's a wonder no one has gotten seriously hurt," she added a moment later.

"I get it," he answered as they resumed their walk uphill. "Any teen worth their salt would want to skate down such a tempting landscape. Though maybe that particular one could have chosen a less crowded time."

Despite his words, he felt a modicum of gratitude for the kid. His daring ride had given Matteo a chance he wouldn't have expected to get. A reason to hold Mari in his arms.

Just. Stop.

Shaking off yet another wayward thought, Matteo followed in her wake.

"We're almost there," she told him over her shoulder.

A few moments later, to his surprise, she turned into what could only be described as a narrow alleyway.

Where in the world was she taking him? They'd passed by numerous fancy-looking restaurants on their way here. But apparently they'd be eating in a small hole-in-the-wall away from the main road.

Finally, Mari stopped in front of a glass door with metallic lettering. *Andiamo's.*

"Not too many people know about this place," she told him as he held the door open for her. "The chef likes to keep it that way. He's not in it for the tourist dollars. Just wants to practice his craft and cook for people he knows will appreciate the food."

Huh. Now that was a novel concept as far as Matteo was concerned. Imagine dedicating your life to a craft and then not being incentivized to make money off your hard-earned skills. Matteo gave a mental shrug at the thought. To each his own. But most of the world didn't work that way.

"A secret for the locals?"

As soon as they stepped inside, myriad aromas tickled his nose. Spices. Tomato sauce. A sweet scent that reminded him of fresh oranges off the tree. The restaurant was most definitely not what he was expecting. It was like stepping into a space/time continuum. They'd entered through a small door off a narrow alleyway. But somehow the inside of the establishment surprisingly vast. Tall ceilings, a wide dining area and a long hallway across the room that seemed to stretch farther down to another part of the establishment. A long wooden bar to the side sported glass shelves packed with dark wine bottles and other spirits.

"You seem surprised," Mari said, a small smile hovering on her lips.

She wasn't wrong. In fact, so far his visit to Cagliari had held one surprise after another.

"This was most certainly not what I was expecting when we turned into that alleyway."

She nodded, flashing him a wide smile. "It's almost magical, isn't it?"

"That's one way to describe it." Another might be to call it an optical illusion.

"Wait till you taste the food. Talk about magical."

"How in the world does the owner keep this place a secret from the tourists?"

"It's in the best interest of the locals to keep the information to themselves."

A slim, tall woman dressed in black slacks and a form-fitting black vest over a white T-shirt approached them, her smile directed at Mari.

"*Bella*, how lovely that you are back. One of the tables in the back okay, as usual?"

"That sounds lovely, Luciana. *Grazie*." She turned to Matteo, then made quick work of introducing him to the hostess. They followed her down the hallway for what seemed like an inordinate amount of time. This place really was an optical illusion. Or maybe Mari was right, there was some type of ancient European magic involved.

As silly as that sounded, Matteo found himself entertaining the thought just a tad longer than reasonable. The illusion only grew stronger when they finally reached the end of the hallway to step out into an outdoor seating area that could only be described as a vast, colorful garden. Bright green bushes and citrus trees ripe with fruit lined the perimeter. Lush, thick grass covered the ground under their feet. The early evening sky cast mild, gray shadows over the landscape. Luciana led them to a round table and another server immediately appeared with full glasses of icy water and plastic-covered menus. She greeted him with a smile and Mari with a few words in Italian.

"You seem to know the staff here well. And you said only locals really know about this place."

"Yes," she answered, taking a sip of her water.

"I take it, then, you spend a lot of time in town?"

She nodded, taking a bite of a piece of bread and swallowing. "Any chance I get. The square reminds me of Faneuil Hall back in Boston. And the rest of the piazza could be the North End, Boston's version of a Little Italy."

So he'd been right about her being a New Englander. "Boston, huh? That's where you're from?"

Another nod. "I grew up in the North End.

In fact, my parents owned a place just like this. Only much, much smaller in scale."

"Why'd you leave?" He was surprised at the question as soon as it left his mouth. But he couldn't help the nagging sense that there was a story there. One he was uncharacteristically curious about.

She looked away, but not before Matteo registered a flash of pain behind her eyes. "It was time to move on to new things. I managed to land a job aboard a cruise ship, which brought me here. And I ended up staying."

That explained the remark she'd made earlier when they'd walked by the big ships. The rest about her was still a big mystery, however. One he desperately wanted to unravel for some reason. "Do you miss it? The States? Your home?"

"Yes and no," Mari answered, taking another bite of her baguette. Clearly she wasn't going to expand on that rather cryptic response.

Matteo wasn't going to push. To any outside observer, they may have appeared to be having a pleasant conversation between two friendly acquaintances, but the reality was that Mari was choosing her sparse words very carefully and giving nothing away. She was guarded, the walls around her nearly tangible. He reminded her of a fawn licking its wounds in solitude.

Was she wounded, then? Had someone hurt her?

That thought had his blood boiling in a way he didn't want to examine.

Mari pulled one of the menus from the center of the table closer to her, began studying it. Clearly an attempt to change the topic. He had no doubt she knew the offerings by heart, given her familiarity with the place.

A server appeared with a tray of antipasto and silently set it down with a smile.

Before he could reach for a morsel of food, Matteo's phone dinged with a message. Glancing at the screen, he bit off a curse.

His father.

"Excuse me," he told her, rising from the table. "I need to take this."

The conversation with his father went about as well as expected. The man was apologetic and regretful. He must have spent another restless night taunted by all the bad decisions he'd made recently. But what good was any of that doing them or Tala Industries? None.

By the time Matteo returned to the table, he was beyond agitated, hoping the upcoming meal would serve to soothe his frazzled nerves.

"You look like you want to throw a plate. We can leave, if you'd like," she offered.

Matteo shook his head. "Not a chance. I'm

famished and this food looks great. My father occasionally needs to get things off his chest, is all."

"Like what?"

Matteo inhaled a deep breath. It wasn't often he spoke of his father, but he found himself wanting to with Mari.

"First he neglected the company, leaving me one hundred percent of the responsibility, and then he let himself be swindled out of most of our wealth. All to please a woman he barely knew. And when it was all gone, so was she."

"Oh, my."

"His reaction to the loss of my mother. In his grief, he sought to find a replacement for her. But he managed to find a con woman instead." The words seemed to be pouring out of him, as if they'd been sitting on his tongue, waiting for the right ears to hear them.

"Matteo, that's dreadful. Your poor father."

Somehow, it didn't surprise him that she'd found sympathy for his foolish papa. He hadn't quite managed to summon the same toward his parent within himself.

She reached for him then, covering his hand with hers. Her palm felt soft, warm against his roughened skin. The contrast sent an unfamiliar sensation through him.

He didn't know how much time passed with the feel of her hand against his before they were interrupted. Two people, a man and a younger-looking woman who appeared to know Mari, approached them after entering the dining room. The young woman smiled politely as they made their way over. The man, on the other hand, looked less than pleased, his gaze shifting from Mari, over to Matteo, then finally resting on their joined hands atop the table. The sight clearly made him unhappy judging by the man's instant frown.

Mari definitely noticed the look as well, as she quickly pulled her hand away and tucked a strand of hair behind her ear.

Whoever this man was, Mari cared what he thought.

A bolt of disappointment sheared through Matteo's gut. Along with another sensation he didn't care to examine.

CHAPTER SIX

SHE REALLY SHOULD have been more prepared to run into someone she knew while at Andiamo's. So it was rather inexcusable that she was caught quite so unprepared and scrambling for words as the two newcomers to the dining room approached their table.

But why did it have to be those particular two? Almost anyone else would have been better. Antonio Giraldi, a professor at Cagliari University, accompanied by one of his American students from Colorado. Catherine was a sweet young lady who had never been anything less than charming to Mari, but she also never passed an opportunity to spread gossip and innuendo.

As for the professor, well, Antonio had expressed his interest in getting to know Mari better more than once. Antonio was always a gentleman and never pushy. Nice enough to look at with a pleasant personality. But Mari had never felt so much as a hint of romantic attraction toward the man in return. Such a shame, really. Being attracted to the professor would be so much more convenient. Antonio wasn't the type of man who would hightail and run when the going got tough like Trevor had. Or the way her mother had decades earlier.

Matteo, on the other hand, struck her as if he very well could be the type who would do just that. After all, he'd thought the worst of her initially, hadn't he?

Not that it mattered. The man was only here for a few more hours.

"Mari?" Antonio asked as they drew closer, his gaze alternating between her and Matteo. Out of reflex, she yanked her hand away out of Matteo's. Both men clearly noticed the hastened action. Matteo tilted his head and Antonio's eyebrows rose half an inch. Luckily, Catherine was too busy closing in on her for a hug to seem to have noticed.

"Mari! So nice to see you here," the other woman exclaimed, throwing her arms around Mari's shoulders. "Who's your friend?" she asked, her eyes fixating on Matteo as soon as she stood. Catherine's expression held no small amount of feminine curiosity.

Mari somehow found her voice enough to

make quick introductions. Matteo stood to shake the professor's hand and flashed a dazzling smile to Catherine, who in turn looked as if she may swoon in reaction.

"I didn't realize Anna had any kin in Italy," Antonio offered, his eyes still assessing Matteo as he sat back down. "Or any at all, for that matter."

"Did you know her well?" Matteo asked.

Antonio nodded. "Fairly well. Anna was a regular fixture in town. Stopped by the university often to bring baked goods or meals to the students. Volunteered her time too. Assisting foreign students get acclimated to the town."

"We all loved her," Catherine added with a solemn nod of her own.

Mari noted the rosy flush of the young woman's cheeks. She seemed to have trouble tearing her gaze from Matteo's face. Who could blame her? The man was strikingly handsome. More than a few female heads had turned in his direction as they'd made their way to the restaurant earlier.

Mari couldn't help but compare the two men before her now. Antonio had classic features that bore tribute to his Roman ancestors. He would be described as attractive by any standard. Crystal-blue eyes, blondish hair with streaks of chestnut brown. A professor of history, his intelligence shone clear in his eyes. He was dedicated to his students and to his chosen field. All that a woman could want and ask for, really.

Just not her.

Her gaze fell to Matteo. In looks, he was the complete opposite of the other man. Dark hair, charcoal black eyes and rugged, sharp features. He was a good three inches taller than Antonio. And while the professor was fit and toned, Matteo clearly had the type of physique that was evidence of hard work and what had to be a punishing fitness routine.

Her thoughts were interrupted by the sound of someone clearing their throat. She couldn't even tell who had done it. Mari snapped her gaze away from Matteo's face. In her dazed distraction, she hadn't even noticed the lull in conversation.

Oh god. Had she been staring at Matteo while the others looked on?

Finally, Antonio broke the silence. "Well, I guess we better head over to our table." He sounded less than enthused about doing so, however.

Catherine nodded in agreement. "Yes, I offered to buy Professor Giraldi dinner in exchange for his gracious offer to assist me with my essay. I'm having the most difficult time writing this one."

Antonio gave her shoulder a reassuring squeeze. "In your defense, it's a rather daunting subject. The influence of ancient Phoenicia on Italian Renaissance art."

"That does sound quite daunting," Mari agreed. "Yes, well. We should let you two get to it, then," she suggested.

Antonio pursed his lips. "Right, then. Guess we'll see you Thursday, Mari."

"I'll be there, as usual."

It was only after the two had walked away that it occurred to her that her statement might have sounded rather rude. The thought was horrifying. What in the world was wrong with her? Something about Matteo was throwing her off and had her acting uncharacteristic and foreign. First getting caught just staring at the man, then making it clearly obvious that she wanted to be alone with him at dinner.

Wait a minute.

That was almost as horrifying as the last thought, in that it was absolutely true. She *did* want to be left alone with Matteo, had grown frustrated and impatient with the interruption of Antonio and Catherine stopping by their table.

Absolutely unacceptable. She hardly knew

the man. And that was the problem in itself. Just how badly she would like to change that. She wanted to know him. In all manner of ways.

What a mess.

"What's Thursday?" Matteo asked, cutting into her disturbing self-revelations. "If you don't mind my asking."

It took a second to register what he was referring to.

"Oh, I volunteer at the university. Facilitating a group study once a week to assist the American students with their Italian. There are several dozen here for the summer, studying abroad for extra credit."

Matteo leaned his forearms over the table. "That's very kind of you. To donate your time in such a way."

"It was Anna's idea."

"Anna is sounding more and more saint-like the more I hear about her."

"She was indeed. I think you would have liked to have known her."

"I'm beginning to realize how true that is. It's truly my loss that I didn't get a chance to make more of an effort to meet her. I'll regret that going forward."

"It wasn't all one-sided. She had regrets too."

He narrowed his eyes on her. "What do you mean?"

A tender spot reserved for Anna rose to the surface of her chest. "Anna told me she wished she might have tried harder to reach out. Both to you and your mother."

At the mention of his parent, Matteo seemed to wince ever so slightly. So slight she might have missed it. He glanced to the side before returning his attention to her. Whatever emotion it was that had been triggered at the mention of his mother, he seemed to have shaken it off.

"She was lucky to have you there with her."

"There was no one else. But I could argue that I was the lucky one."

He flashed her a knowing smile. "I bet you would, Mari."

As tired and jet-lagged as he felt, Matteo really should have suggested they end the evening after dinner and that he finally get some rest. But he didn't want this time with Mari to end. There was so much more he wanted to ask her. Not just about the hotel and Anna, but also about her past. What exactly had brought her here? Why were there no clues about her previous home in her current one?

What was the deal between her and that professor?

Not that any of it was any of his business. Particularly that last question.

Still, he was trying to come up with an excuse to suggest prolonging the evening a while longer when she luckily took the matter into her own hands.

"I should probably walk some of this off," she said, gesturing to the now-empty pizza platter sitting in the center of the table and the various other mostly eaten dishes surrounding it. As good as Mari had said this restaurant was, her words hadn't been able to do the place justice. The roasted branzino was so fresh he would guess it had been caught just this morning. The pizza and vodka-sauce-soaked homemade pasta had both been works of culinary art. All of it followed by a melt-in-your-mouth limoncello cake with mixed berry drizzle.

"It will have to be a very slow walk. After all that food."

She nodded solemnly. "Really slow," she agreed. "Especially seeing as we're going further uphill." She pointed toward the ceiling.

Matteo released a low groan, only half joking.

Mari laughed at his reaction, her eyes twinkling with amusement. "It will be worth it. The view from the top of this hill is breathtaking. Trust me."

"I do trust you," he told her, the words surprising him as they left his mouth at how true and correct they were. A rather surprising turn of events. Not to mention unexpected and quick.

He didn't often put his trust in others so easily.

He'd already shared more about his father with Mari than anyone else ever. And he'd met the woman less than twenty-four hours ago.

Not like he knew anything about the woman really. Yet, he'd shared one of the most personal, shameful parts of his past with her just now at dinner. A part he'd rather hide from the world. As of yet, the business world knew Tala Industries' financial troubles only to be the result of poor management and fiscal irresponsibility. No one had yet scratched the surface to uncover that the source of that mismanagement had been due to his father's arduous interests that had him falling for a con woman. The news reports that would be generated if the truth was uncovered made Matteo shudder.

Thinking of Tala triggered a reminder of why he was here in the first place. Instead of pouring his soul out to Mari about his father's mistakes and their tragic results, he should have been gently proposing taking over the hotel from her. But at the moment, he couldn't seem to bring himself to even broach the subject. The evening and dinner were much too pleasurable. He didn't want to mar the experience in any way.

"Let's start that walk, then, shall we?" he said, signing the bill and standing. Suddenly, he found he was eager to get outside into the fresh air, his mind in need of clearing.

As they made their exit, they passed the table where Mari's friends sat with their heads over a tablet. The gentleman, Antonio, snapped his head up and gave them an intense perusing stare as they passed by, and Mari waved. The young lady flashed a wide smile, her eyes landing square on Matteo.

Mari turned to him as soon as they stepped outside, a knowing look in her eyes.

"What?" he asked.

"I get the feeling I'm going to get a lot of questions about you when I step into the classroom on Thursday. From Catherine."

"Just Catherine? Antonio looked plenty curious himself about what you were doing having dinner with me."

The gentle smile on her face faltered. "Yes, well. Antonio can ask too, I suppose."

They began walking toward the main pathway. Matteo found he couldn't stop himself from asking the next question. "Is it his business to know?"

It took Mari a moment to answer. "Who I choose to have dinner with is my business and mine alone. I don't have to answer to anyone."

Anymore. The word may have been unspoken but it was as clear as the evening sky.

As relieved as Matteo was about her response regarding the professor, he felt that same tug of ire in his chest. Someone had clearly hurt Mari. He'd suspected so but now he had no doubt. It really was none of his business. How many times did he have to remind himself of that fact since meeting her? So why was he so vexed and angry about it on her behalf?

"Do you want to talk about it?"

"About Antonio? He's a close friend."

It was hard to tell whether she'd intentionally misinterpreted his question. And even harder to guess exactly what she meant by "close."

Again. None of his business. Like she'd said a mere moment ago, whom she chose to spend time with was her business alone.

He would just have to keep reminding himself of that too.

What had she been thinking? There'd been absolutely no reason for her to suggest prolonging this evening by asking Matteo to take a walk with her after dinner.

She was no doubt going to regret this come tomorrow. Though acting on impulse had worked out pretty well for her more than once in the past. Like the series of events that had led her to Cagliari in the first place.

Something told her that impulsiveness when it came to a man like Matteo wouldn't work out quite so well. Not for her, anyway.

They made their way up past the shops and restaurants until the road narrowed and the modern structures gave way to older resident buildings and a cobblestone road.

A few minutes later, they'd reached the grassy area Mari considered one of her favorite places on the island, if not the entire world. High atop the hill, with a breathtaking view of the skyline in the distance, the park had to be the most relaxing spot on the planet. Rosemary bushes that framed its perimeter lent a subtle scent of the herb, adding to the ambience.

"Wow. That's quite a view," Matteo commented. "And it sort of smells like we're still in the restaurant."

"Very observant. Here, I'll show you." She led him to the nearest bush and plucked a few leaves and popped them into her mouth.

Matteo stared at her as she chewed. "Those are edible?"

She nodded. "Unless, for some reason you have an aversion to rosemary."

"This is rosemary?"

"Yes. It grows wild throughout the island," she answered. Then seemingly without thinking, she raised her hand to his mouth to offer him the rest. His eyebrows rose about an inch, leading her to realize exactly what she'd done. Before she could snatch her hand away, he reached for it, gently wrapping his fingers around her wrist. Then his lips were on her palm, taking the remaining leaves into his mouth. A bolt of lightning shot through her core at the contact, leaving a scorching heat in its wake. Several heavy moments passed where neither one of them spoke, the world around them seeming to disappear. She could only stand still and watch as he slowly chewed, his eyes locked on hers, his warm hand wrapped around her skin. So intimate. Lifting her hand to his mouth had come as naturally to her as bringing the leaves to her own lips to taste.

The thought brought yet more heat to her center. She imagined those lips on hers, the way he would taste right now with the rosemary leaves upon his tongue. How it would feel to taste him.

Just stop.

Mari gave herself a mental shake and pushed the illicit thoughts away.

Finally, she somehow found the wherewithal to come to her senses and gently pull her hand away. Matteo sucked in a sharp breath. Was he as affected by what had just happened as she was? Did he even notice the charged air between them? Maybe she was imagining all of it.

Struggling to find her voice, she finally managed to tear her gaze away from his and motion to the horizon. "Wait till you see the view from up here. Follow me."

Without waiting for an answer or a reaction, she turned on her heel and walked to the other end of the park to the rock wall ledge that overlooked the majestic scene beyond. She could sense Matteo less than a foot behind her. He audibly gasped when he reached her side. The stunning buildings and structures of the town below them spread out toward the brilliant blue of the ocean. Just beyond the water was the looming rocky Isola de Cavoli, a small island within boating distance. She could only imagine Matteo's reaction at seeing all this. The first time she'd come upon this view, she'd felt as if she'd walked up to a massive painting that had somehow come to life.

"It's like nothing I've seen before," he said next to her, the awe in his voice sharp and clear.

She could say the same.

"You haven't seen anything yet. Just watch, the sun's about to set."

Matteo draped his forearms over the rock wall and crossed his wrists. Mari found herself studying him from the side, hoping he wouldn't notice. He seemed wholly focused on the scene before him. All sharp angles and dark features. The way he was postured as he watched the sun begin to set, everything about the man screamed masculinity. Against this backdrop, he might have stepped right out of a cologne ad in some high-end magazine. She made herself look away before he turned and caught her staring. How horrifying that would be.

When she'd first sent those emails to the mysterious relative Anna had told her about, it hadn't even occurred to her that she'd be standing next to him after dinner one night fighting a wholly inconvenient physical pull unlike she'd ever felt toward any man.

Several moments passed in silence, as they simply watched the explosion of colors before them. A brilliant shade of red with streaks of dark orange. The pole lights around the park began to light within moments of the sun's descent. The brightest stars began to twinkle above them.

Matteo turned to her, his smile wide. "Thank you for bringing me here. It's been a while since I was able to simply stop and appreciate my surroundings."

His words brought an inordinate amount of pleasure to her heart. Then she noticed the deep sorrow in his eyes. His father. He'd mentioned earlier in the restaurant that his parent had been a source of turmoil in his life.

"Do you want to talk about it?"

He gave a casual shrug of his shoulder but a wealth of emotion washed through his eyes. "It's a common enough story. My father didn't know what to do with his grief after the loss of my mother. So he left himself open to be used by the first woman who showed him any interest." Matteo continued staring off into the distance as he continued. "A woman who happened to be the furthest in resemblance to my mother as imaginably possible." He released a small chuckle that held no mirth. "That might be the funniest part in all of this. He thought he could replace his wife of thirty years with the likes of *her*." The last word held so much disdain, Mari felt as if she might be able to touch it in the air.

Matteo gave a shake of his head. "Enough of

all this sad talk. No need to mar what's been a highly enjoyable evening so far, is there?"

As far as changing the subject, it was a rather effective attempt. She wasn't going to push. Heaven knew, she didn't really want to discuss the parts of her past that had brought her so much pain either.

"Let's head back toward town. We'll take another way down."

He lifted an eyebrow. "Oh?"

She smiled at him. "There are some girls I'd like to visit. I stop by to see them whenever I come here."

"Girls?"

"A few boys too."

His eyebrows furrowed in confusion. The man really was good-looking when he was perplexed. And at all other times too, actually.

Mari chuckled at his expression. "You'll see." Taking his arm, she led him to the other side of the park to the stone stairway that led about halfway down the hill to her intended destination.

"Right there." She pointed to a small alcove off to the side. Nestled under the overhanging branches of a downy oak tree was a five-foot-tall structure complete with pet beds and a tall scratching post. Bowls full of food and water sat at the grassy base. "Good. Looks like most of them are here."

Matteo shifted his gaze from the sight before him, to Mari's face and back again. "Kittens. Your boys and girls are kittens. They're who you come to visit when you come here."

She nodded. "That's right. They're all complete sweethearts."

One of those sweethearts, perhaps the smallest of the litter, jumped down from her ledge and made her way to where Matteo stood. She nestled her nose against his ankle, purring softly.

"She likes you," Mari announced.

"Huh." Matteo stared at the little feline as if he was seeing a cat for the very first time. Then he bent down and picked it up, brought her up to his face. "Hello, little one."

"That one's called Dante," Mari informed him.

He brought the kitten closer to his face and rubbed his cheek against its soft fur. Dante meowed with clear contentment. Mari had to look away, the image of Matteo handling a small cat with such gentleness and affection doing something to her center that felt both alien and raw.

How did he manage to look so masculine and rugged snuggling a small kitten to his chest?

"I don't think I've ever held a kitten before,"

he told her, nuzzling Dante some more. "I've only ever had dogs growing up. Much bigger than little Dante here."

Inexperienced or not, he certainly seemed to know what he was doing, holding Dante like a fragile piece of glass, nuzzling against his whiskers softly. Even though the kitten looked like a tiny toy in Matteo's large hands, Matteo seemed to be a natural at handling it.

"Just FYI though, Dante can be a little temperamental."

Even before she got the last words out, the little rascal let out a surprisingly loud screech and jumped out of Matteo's hands. It landed deftly on its feet. Along the way, he swiped a sharp claw against the top of Matteo's hand. The resulting scratch was immediate and angry. Matteo barely noticed, fixated on the kitten now at his feet who had just jumped out his arms but seemed intent currently to climb back up his leg.

"I think he's telling you he'd like to go back to bed now."

Matteo bent and picked Dante up once more.

Mari stepped over to them and studied the ragged scratch on the top of Matteo's hand. "Uh-oh. Might want to watch yourself for any strange symptoms."

He lifted an eyebrow in question. "Symptoms?"

Mari wrangled a serious expression over her features. "You never know with outdoor animals. Wouldn't want you coming down with rabies. Or something worse."

He grew a shade paler. "Worse than rabies?"

She nodded solemnly. "I mean, rabies is bad enough. Agonizingly painful and the symptoms come on instantaneously."

Matteo grew a shade paler at her words. She just couldn't do it to him any longer, worrying him in such a way. "I'm only teasing you, rabies is considered nonexistent in Sardinia." Still, she couldn't resist adding, "Fleas, on the other hand..."

Matteo paused in his handling of the furry creature he held. "What?"

Mari could barely suppress the laughter hovering in her chest or the twitching of her lips. She knew for a fact each of these cats was tended to with proper medication and administered all necessary preventatives.

Matteo gave her a stern look. "Ha, ha. Very funny."

Walking back to the structure, he gently placed the squirming feline on one of the empty beds. The tiny creature let out a squeaky meow in protest at being put away but then snuggled into the soft material and promptly closed its eyes. The image struck Mari in a part of her she hadn't acknowledged in a long time. She'd vowed not to acknowledge that part of her after Trevor. And had no business doing so now, especially because of the man before her. Still, the way Matteo looked right now, gently handling the kitten with such care and affection, had the coldness within her core beginning to melt.

Oh, she really had to be careful here. Mari made herself look away when Matteo gave the tiny cat another soft scratch under its chin. But the picture remained hanging in her mind like a portrait. She recalled the way Catherine had looked at Matteo back at the restaurant, all the feminine stares that had been directed at him as they'd walked up the hill and climbed the steps. The man had a scorching appeal and if she wasn't cautious, she might very well get burned.

CHAPTER SEVEN

Morning arrived much too early the next day. Or perhaps Mari just felt that way because she'd only recently drifted off to sleep. A restless sleep at that. Thoughts of Matteo had kept intruding on her attempts to reach slumber. The expression on his face as they'd watched the sunset together. Funny, she'd seen the sun setting from that vantage point countless times since she'd arrived in Sardinia, but the view last night had seemed almost magical.

Even against such a dreamlike backdrop, the hurt in Matteo's voice when he'd spoken of his father had resonated deep within her core. She had to wonder if he'd gotten a chance to grieve for his own loss due to having to deal with his father's behavior. Heaven knew, she was still grieving the loss of her own father. Losing Papa had caused a wound in her soul that would never heal. At least Matteo had another parent to share the pain with, despite their clearly strained current relationship. At least Matteo's other parent hadn't abandoned him, unlike Mari's mother.

Now, it was hard to reconcile the man who'd held Dante gently up against his chin with the one who had arrived yesterday morning with all that bluster and insult. The first impression he'd given her of himself had been almost reproachful, with the way he'd accused her of taking advantage of Anna.

Perhaps that first version of Matteo was the preferable one. She was far too attracted to the version from last night.

There were definitely layers to the man she wouldn't have guessed upon meeting him that first time. The way he'd held little Dante so gently in his large hands replayed like a movie in her mind. How would those hands feel against her own skin? What would it feel like to have him nuzzle his cheek against hers that way?

Whoa, boy. She gave herself a mental thwack. Thoughts like that were nothing but dangerous for her sanity. Fantasizing about a man was entirely a foreign concept for her. No reason to start now.

Only there was, wasn't there? The reason happened to be six feet tall, devastatingly handsome and happened to have spent the night in her hotel.

So close and yet so far.

Great, now she was waxing poetic. How utterly pathetic of her.

Mari rubbed a palm down her face. Enough of that. She had an establishment to run. Signore Gio would no doubt demand some of her time after she'd been gone all last evening. And there was something pressing on today's schedule, she was certain. What was it? For the life of her she couldn't recall.

She didn't have it in her just yet to retrieve her phone from the bedside and call up her calendar. Whatever was on her itinerary would become clear soon enough. Mari would tackle it right after she took a shower and downed perhaps a pitcher of Esmerelda's espresso. Maybe she'd run into Matteo in the dining area. Was he up already? How had he found his room? Hopefully, it had been to his liking. It wasn't one of the hotel's high-end suites but was cozy enough with a striking view of the beach and ocean. Maybe he was at his balcony staring at the view right at this moment.

Stop that! Stop thinking about him already. Sure, the two of them seemed to have made some sort of connection yesterday at dinner and then during the walk afterward. But last evening was just…a brief interlude. Who knew when the man was going to be back in Sardinia. He was just here to look into the parcel of land Anna had left him. Then he'd go back to his life in Rome and would probably not even bother to visit the island again.

He'd go on with his life and she would have to go on with hers. Funny, forty-eight hours ago, that prospect would have been just fine with her. She was more than content with her current lot in life. She lived and worked in paradise. Her job was fulfilling, and she was good at it. A volunteer gig at the local university brought her into contact with diverse and enigmatic young students from all over the world. Sure, she missed Anna and would do so forever. But she was lucky to have had the older woman in her life to begin with. Anna had been more family to her than the blood kin who'd made her final days in Boston the nightmare that she'd had to run away from four years ago.

As far as a love life… Well, she couldn't even go there. Not in her mind and not in reality. Getting over the way Trevor had treated her was going to be a lifelong endeavor. She'd thought he'd loved her, that he would stand by her. Instead, he'd dumped her and ran when her life was thrown into turmoil by her uncle. He'd never come out and said so, but Mari had seen the suspicion in Trevor's eyes when her uncle had made his accusations. She could tell he'd begun to realize that what his parents had been saying about her being beneath him might be true, after all. Trevor had never actually admitted to believing her uncle's lies. She might have even respected his decision to walk away if he had.

Instead, he'd taken the easy way out. Told her he couldn't handle the turmoil in her life.

Too complicated. Those were Trevor's exact words. Like the possibility of being charged with a crime was nothing more than an inconvenience.

Mari scoffed out loud. He'd been right, hadn't he? He'd simply walked away rather than help her deal with it all.

Thoughts of those dark days threatened to shadow her spirit for hours if she entertained them at all. Instead, she made herself focus on the melodic birdsong faintly echoing from outside her window and the soft crashing waves of the ocean that one could hear if their ears strained enough. Several deep breaths later, she tossed the covers aside finally and scrambled out of bed.

The steamy hot shower served to jostle the remaining lingering unwanted thoughts from her mind and she felt lighter and calmer as she made her way downstairs to the lobby.

Miyko stood at the front desk and gave her a scrutinizing look when she approached.

"You were gone late last night," he said, his gaze roaming the length of her. "For you anyway," he added. "You're usually in bed by nine at the latest."

She ignored the speculative comments. He was clearly fishing for information about her time spent with Matteo. She had no inclination to give him any. "Good morning, Miyko. And how are you today?"

"Bene, grazie," he answered. *"E tu?"*

"Bene. Though I'll be much better once I get some of Esme's espresso."

Miyko's eyes followed her as she headed toward the coffee bar. "Well, don't take too long. The rep from the excursion company is due to arrive within half an hour."

Mari paused in her tracks. A curse escaped her lips. That was the engagement she'd been spacing on. They were due to experience one of their excursion offerings firsthand.

"Oh, and I won't be able to accompany you, after all. Mama is not feeling too well. I'll have to stay here and man the desk."

"Is Roberta okay?"

Miyko waved his hand dismissively. "She just overindulged at dinner last night. Chef made his rich and heavy lasagna."

Mari's concern for the older woman was quickly displaced with frustration at what her absence would mean for her schedule today.

"I can hardly go by myself. They've made accommodations and prepared food for at least two people."

Matteo chose that moment to step out of the elevator. Miyko's eyes lit up with mischief at the sight of him.

Mari could just guess where his thoughts had led. *Oh no.*

"You don't have to, Mari. I have an excellent idea."

He nodded in Matteo's direction.

It had been a while since Matteo had needed a cold shower in the morning to start the day. That's what happened when a man's dreams overnight kept featuring a dark-haired, doe-eyed beauty who had him thinking wicked thoughts about her all night.

Knowing she slept only a few floors below made the yearnings all that much stronger. So close yet so far.

Sitting on the edge of the comfortable mattress in a damp towel around his waist this morning, Matteo wondered if he'd stayed under the cold spray long enough. A lingering heat still curled at the base of his center. More than once last night, he'd fantasized about what it would feel like to kiss her, to hold her in his arms. What her reaction might be if he found his way to her room and knocked on her door. Would she let him in, greet him with bated breath and longing the same way he longed for her?

Not that his wayward thoughts were any of Mari's fault.

No, it was all his doing that he couldn't get her out of his mind after they'd returned to their respective rooms last night. They were mere acquaintances who'd just met. But last night might have been one of the most picture-book-perfect evenings he'd spent with a woman. Even riding on a city bus with Mari was somehow notable and romantic.

If only circumstances between them could have been different. If only he wasn't here to see about acquiring control of the hotel and the land it sat on.

A surge of guilt made him wince internally. Such a useless emotion, guilt. A luxury he couldn't afford. He had a business to rebuild and right now, this hotel was the only clear path to begin that endeavor.

How utterly troublesome that he was so attracted to her.

Last night should not have happened, he shouldn't have enjoyed it so much. He'd meant to at least broach the subject of taking over the hotel from her, yet he'd never gotten around to it. That was unacceptable. Right now, he should be back in Rome at his office trying to figure out what his next steps should be.

Had he really been playing with a kitten? The dull ache of the small scratch at the top of his hand was proof that he indeed had.

More importantly, had he really shared so much about his difficulties with his father and about the loss of his mother? It was as if someone else had entered his body and discussed all those things with Mari.

By contrast, he knew next to nothing about her. He had no real idea about her past. What had driven her from the cobblestoned sidewalks of Boston to the shores of Sardinia? What exactly was her story?

She certainly didn't seem inclined to share the way he had. Well, no more. From now on, whenever he interacted with Mari, he would be a closed book. Just like her.

If he was smart, he'd try to avoid her altogether until the next flight back to Rome this evening. In the meantime, he had to get dressed and find some breakfast and much-needed caffeine.

Stepping out of the elevator into the lobby moments later, he sensed Mari's presence before he saw or heard her. So much for trying to avoid the woman for his sanity's sake.

The employee who manned the front desk—Miyko was his name?—flashed him a curious smile. Mari's focus was on the other man, shooting daggers at him with her eyes.

"I think Signore Talarico should join you today, Mari," Miyko was saying.

Join her for what exactly?

He was about to direct the question out loud to Mari but her expression had turned downright murderous. He could practically see steam rising out of her. Her ire was directed straight at her employee. If looks could kill, the man would be growing cold on the tile floor right about now. Miyko, for his part, didn't seem to notice Mari's discomfort. In fact, he appeared to be enjoying himself.

Miyko crossed his arms in front of his chest and directed his next comments to Matteo. "You see, Mari and I were supposed to go on an introductory excursion by one of the hotel's outside partners. A limo ride to the harbor, followed by a sail on a pirate ship to a tiny island with a historic lighthouse. They're trying to sell us their services."

Huh. What did any of that have to do with him?

Miyko continued, answering that very question. "Turns out I can't go. I have to stay here and man the desk. You should go with Mari in my place."

Mari's eyes grew wide. She stepped over to the desk. She cleared her throat nervously before beginning. "On the other hand, the two of you could go. And I can stay here and mind the desk."

Miyko shook his head slowly. "That makes no sense. We need to see how the excursion might be experienced by both our male and female guests."

Mari sucked in a breath. "But I'm sure Signore Talarico has other things he needs to do. I'm guessing he's much too busy to waste away the day with such things."

Ouch. Matteo was trying hard not to be offended at just how strongly Mari felt about not going on this little trek with him.

"Actually, I'm totally free until my flight later this evening."

Mari's jaw fell as she turned to him. She seemed to be scrambling for what to say next as she worked her jaw up and down.

"I've never been sailing on a pirate ship before," he added.

That was true enough. He was more than a little curious about that leg of the trip in particular. It wasn't as if he had anything better to do before his flight. And he was rather curious about what else the island had to offer after the experiences of last night.

Right. As if that's the only reason, a faint voice teased him from the back recesses of his mind.

Matteo pushed it away before it could grow any louder.

Matteo tended to keep a spare pair of swim trunks in the bottom of his carry-on luggage. He'd never actually needed them until today. Good thing too. He didn't think Miyko's clothing would fit him very well. And there was no doubt the other man would have offered to let Matteo borrow a pair. He seemed very intent on making sure Matteo was able to go on this excursion with Mari.

Mari, on the other hand...

Sure, Miyko was absolutely playing him as some sort of pawn. The game seemed to be forcing Mari's hand and trying to embarrass her. Maybe it was some kind of employee/boss power play. Or maybe Miyko was just a mischievous trickster who liked to watch others squirm in discomfort.

Or all of the above.

Whatever the case, Matteo didn't see a way to back out of the trip now after he'd already said yes. Besides, he really did want to go.

"I'll just go get my things," he said, ignoring the look of utter defeat on Mari's face.

What was so wrong about the prospect of spending the day with him anyhow? After all, they'd had a good time yesterday together, hadn't they? Why did she look horrified at having to be with him again?

Silly question.

The answer was the same reason that he should have declined the offer to go. Hadn't he himself just a few moments ago upstairs in his room decided that last night had been a mistake? Hadn't he vowed to stay away from Mari because of how attracted he was to her?

His resolve sure hadn't lasted long. About the

length of time it took him to get downstairs and lay eyes on her again.

Well, if he was going to spend the day with her, he definitely had to be more careful about exactly where his thoughts led.

Miyko glanced at his watch. "Yes, go get your things, Signore Talarico. The car should be arriving in a few minutes to pick you two up."

Just like that, it was a done deal. Matteo nodded. "I'll be right back."

She was already at the curb when he made his way back downstairs, standing in front of a sleek, black sedan so highly polished that the sun reflecting off its surface had him squinting. She looked as if she'd rather be anywhere else.

She also looked lovely. In the short period of time they'd been apart, Mari had somehow pulled herself together as if she'd had hours. Her hair sat in some kind of complicated-twist bun atop her head that left several delicate tendrils loose, framing her face, the loose hair blowing against her skin in the soft breeze. She wore a colorful printed wrap dress that hung to her curves in all the right ways. The amber hue brought out the golden tone of her tanned skin. On her feet were delicate sensible sandals with straps that wrapped around her ankles and showed off her neon-painted toes.

Great. Now, he was noticing her toes again.

She looked like a picture out of an advertisement for European island living. Except for the scowl on her face.

Matteo went from feeling offended to amused. She really was feeling put out about this whole thing. Would Miyko see a dock in his pay? Was Mari the petty vengeful type?

Perhaps her vengeance would be directed at Matteo for accepting the invitation.

His amusement grew. No other woman had ever had him guessing and wondering about them quite so before. Mari felt like a puzzle he needed to figure out.

A driver emerged from the other side of the car and greeted him in Italian. An older gentleman with a friendly smile and crisp uniform, he looked straight out of central casting if the director needed an Italian chauffeur.

He opened the back door for them and Matteo motioned Mari inside. With a loud, resigned sigh, Mari sat inside the car and scooted over to the other side. She flashed the driver a friendly smile along the way. Something told Matteo that would be one of the few smiles gracing her lips today. With a low chuckle, he joined her inside the car.

His amusement faded quickly once he sat

down in the car seat next to her. The sedan wasn't quite as roomy as it looked from the outside. A tinted glass partition separated them from the driver in the front seat. So they'd essentially be alone together, in tight quarters for who knew what amount of time. He really should have asked more questions about this excursion.

"How long before we get there?"

"We're heading to the other side of the island. It's about a two-and-a-half-hour ride," she answered, sounding not terribly happy about it.

Okay. That wasn't so bad. He could do a bit over two hours. He could ignore the sheen of her skin, the scent of her berry shampoo, the urge to brush one of those wayward tendrils off her cheek.

But then she shifted to place her bag by her feet and her bare knee brushed against his leg. The contact had heat shooting through his thigh and then higher. Matteo gripped his fingers tight against his palm to keep from reaching for her, rubbing his hand against that tempting, tanned and shapely knee.

Mari seemed unaware of the slight contact. And why wouldn't she be? It was barely a whisper of a touch. Yet it elicited a physical reaction within him that he felt deep in his core.

So maybe he was wrong about being able to handle over two hours alone with Mari in the car. They'd barely been in the back seat for a full minute and already he was hyperaware of how attracted he was to her.

Matteo watched out the window as the buildings and hotels of the city gave way to rural, grassy hills and rambling fields. The first part of the ride passed mostly in silence, except for the soft notes of the Spanish guitar music the driver had piping through the vehicle. Matteo had half a mind to ask him to switch to another playlist. Something about the notes brought to mind slow dancing closely with a partner, and the atmosphere felt too romantic for comfort.

Mari's next words definitely reset that vibe.

"Did you itch much last night?" she asked him. "I don't see you scratching."

That question was definitely not romantic in the least. "Itch? Why would I itch?"

He remembered then the way she'd teased him yesterday about handling the kitten. "Ha, ha. Very funny. I don't have fleas."

She shrugged. "We can only hope. Sometimes it takes a day or two to manifest their symptoms." Her tone was serious enough, but Matteo didn't miss the small tug at the corner of her mouth to keep from laughing.

"I don't have fleas," he repeated. But darned if he didn't feel a slight itchy sensation along his skin below his left knee. No way he was going to give her the satisfaction of scratching at it. He was positive it wasn't any kind of insect bite. Mari was just getting back at him about agreeing to go on this trip. The chances he had a fleabite were astronomically low.

Weren't they?

"You know," he began, turning in his seat to fully face her. "I don't think Dante infected me with bloodsucking parasites, but if I went back there and the little critter tried climbing up my pant leg, I'd lift him up again."

She raised a delicately arched eyebrow. "Is that so?"

He nodded. "Yes. In fact, there's nothing about yesterday that I'd do any differently."

Whoa. He hadn't meant to utter such a double entendre. Surprisingly, he meant what he'd just said. Mari sat staring at him, her mouth agape now. His words or their meaning were not lost on her.

Scrambling to fill the heavy air and just to have something to say, Matteo pointed out the window at the field they were passing, not even certain what he was looking at.

"Those have got to be the funniest-looking dogs I've ever seen."

Mari blinked up at him, confusion flooding her features at the sudden change of topic. Eventually, she moved her gaze to where he pointed.

A chuckle escaped her lips as soon as she did. "Those are not dogs, Matteo."

Matteo squinted, turning his head, but the vehicle was traveling too fast to get another good look. "What were they, then?"

"You need to get out of the city more," she told him, amusement dancing in her dark eyes.

"Why?"

"That's what sheep look like when they've been shorn of their wool."

"Huh. Who knew? I guess I do need to get out to the country more often."

Mari's' chuckle erupted into all-out, full-on laughter. Matteo found it was impossible not to laugh along with her.

And just like that, the tension between them broke. As if it had never been there.

It was really too bad that she was going to have to fire Miyko as soon as they got back to the hotel. She'd never actually agreed to go along with any of this. Though, truth be told, Mari probably could have fought harder to say no.

Frankly, she'd been surprised that Matteo had even agreed so readily to come along. Miyko hadn't even tried to persuade or bamboozle him the way he'd done with her. Go figure. Mari would have absolutely pegged him as more of an eighteen-hole-golf-followed-by-cocktails-then-dinner-party type rather than the sort who'd be interested in a pirate-themed daylong boating excursion.

Matteo Talarico had managed to throw her one curve after another since he'd arrived on this island. She was done trying to figure him out.

Well, now that she was here, she may as well try and enjoy herself. Plus, she had to admit it— Matteo made her laugh. She couldn't remember the last time she'd said that about a man. Or that she'd done much laughing at all, for that matter.

Now, as the car came to a stop at the marina, Mari exited the car and took a moment to ground herself. It was going to be a long day, spent mostly alone with Matteo. The warm glow of the sun, along with the soft breeze drifting off the water, served to further temper her mood. This wasn't so bad. Maybe Miyko would be keeping his job after all. Matteo joined her by the side of the car, stretching his arms up toward the sky. She caught a peek of a toned and tanned stomach as his T-shirt lifted at the waist. She sharply tore her gaze away. If this day was going to go smoothly at all, she had to stop doing things like that. Like noticing his taut stomach. Or the way the warm sun brought out the lighter streaks in his dark hair. Or how enthusiastic he looked at the moment.

Right. She was going to stop all that. Starting now.

The driver came over and explained the exact time and spot that someone would be back to pick them up. Matteo shook the man's hand and she didn't miss that he slipped a couple of bills into his palm in the process.

Mari bid the driver goodbye as another couple of gentlemen approached them with wide smiles and greetings in Italian. Her accent when responding must have given her away as an American because they immediately switched to flawless English.

"Welcome to you both!" said the blond one with the bright hazel eyes. "I'm Franco and this is Stavi. We're your tour guides. Are you ready to start your adventure?"

Mari nodded, though she was far from certain.

CHAPTER EIGHT

THE DAY COULDN'T have been better suited for them. Stepping out of the vehicle, Matteo took a moment to take in his surroundings. The sun shone a bright golden yellow, reflecting off the soft ripples of the water. Boats and ships of all sizes dotted the square dock. Nautical flags surrounded the larger Italian il Tricolore atop the three-structure building. The soft breeze occasionally gave way to a stronger gust that sent the aroma of the sea drifting in the air.

An adventure. That's what the tour guide had called it. Sure, he was trying to sell this outing to Mari so she'd offer it at her hotel to her guests, but Matteo could see how the excursion would be a popular draw to tourists and locals alike. Look how readily he'd jumped on the chance to go. He didn't often act on impulse. But saying yes this morning had definitely been impulsive.

Maybe it was meant to be that he be here.

When was the last time he did anything just for the hell of it? Just to enjoy himself, have a little fun? Even the party-like events he often attended were business related.

Maybe this entire week was meant to be. Fated somehow. The call from his lawyer. Then traveling to Cagliari.

Meeting Mari.

Maybe he was meant to know her. To get a touch of some lighthearted fun that included watching a sunset atop a majestic hill, petting a soft-furred kitten, sailing on a pirate ship. All in the company of a beautiful woman who seemed to draw out a side of him he hadn't known existed.

Too bad it was all so temporary. Too bad she was no doubt going to dislike him when he finally confessed as to his real motives.

The idea sent a sinking feeling in his chest. It bothered him that Mari would think less of him at some undeniable point in the future.

A blur of motion caught the side of his eye, pulling him out of his unpleasant musings. He looked down to see a small child approaching the two of them. A girl dressed in a colorful frock, carrying a basket. She held it up to Mari, then swung it in his direction. "Fig!" she exclaimed. *"Per te,"* she added.

A frazzled petite blond woman was fast on her heels. *"Scusa,"* she said, in a flustered tone. "She's very excited about the figs she picked at her grandfather's garden. I'm sorry she's intruded."

"That's all right," Mari immediately answered, reaching inside the offered basket. "I'd love a fig, *grazie*."

The mother gave Mari a relieved smile. "You've made her very happy." She glanced from Mari's face to Matteo. "Do you two have any of your own?" she asked, just as Mari took a bite of the gifted fruit. She sputtered at the question just as its exact meaning registered in Matteo's head. The mother thought they were a couple who possibly had children. No wonder Mari appeared near ready to spit out her fig.

They both immediately began denying the woman's assumption in unison.

"Oh, we're not—" Mari began, mumbling through her mouthful.

Just as Matteo shook his head, saying "No, that's not…"

The woman seemed to realize her mistake, though her expression was one of tickled amusement. "Ah, I see," she said, gathering her daughter about the shoulders and turning her around. "Pardon my mistake."

Matteo watched the two figures walk away, wracking his brain for what in the world he might say to Mari next. She had to feel as awkward as he did.

He cleared his throat before beginning. No sense in ignoring the proverbial elephant between them. "It's an innocent enough mistake on her part."

Mari quickly nodded. She was clearly at a loss, too, for she simply held up the fruit in her hand. "Want a bite? It's quite fresh."

She immediately dropped her hand before waiting for an answer, her cheeks flushing a ruby red. Yet another innocent remark that was actually quite loaded. Mari clearly came to the same realization as soon as she'd said the words.

Matteo did his best not to groan out loud. The thought of reaching for her hand, pulling the fig up to his own lips, taking a bite from the spot her lips had just touched had lightning bolts shooting up his center.

Blessedly, Stavi chose that moment to announce that their transport boat had arrived to sail them to the bigger ship farther out at sea.

"We'll be serving some light refreshments on board," he told them. "To stave off your hunger until lunch on the beach later."

Lunch on the beach. That sounded…quite romantic. Matteo had to suppress yet another groan. He gave his head a mental shake, focusing on the here and now. They were boarding a boat. Mari was taking her shoes off and handing them to Stavi, who placed them carefully in a plastic container. Then he reached his hand out to her. Matteo didn't even think of what he was doing; if anyone was going to help Mari onto this watercraft, it was going to be him. Taking her hand and gently wrapping his other arm around her waist, he gently guided her onto the first step. There was nothing for it, the woman felt natural in his arms. Touching her felt natural, innate. As if he'd been doing so his whole life. As if he never should stop.

He could only hope Mari didn't notice how his hands lingered about her waist, how he hesitated letting go of her.

Once Mari was on board and had moved onto the seat, he followed her lead and took his own loafers off and handed them to Stavi before boarding himself. The other man gave him a knowing smile as he descended onto the boat, followed by a quick blink of an eye.

Matteo wasn't going to try and interpret what any of it might mean.

Mari settled into the plush leather bucket seat portside and pushed her sunglasses farther up her nose. The feel of Matteo's palms against her skin through her thin dress had her senses tingling. Good thing he had been holding her; she'd nearly lost her balance at the unexpected contact. She tried to take her mind off how good it had felt to be held by him by concentrating on the spectacular view.

Not a cloud in sight, the sky was a brilliant blue that could have come off a paint palette. A gray mountain loomed far ahead in the distance, the water clear and deep beneath them. A picture-perfect scene, really. As much as she liked Miyko—well, most of the time she did—sitting here with her employee would not have held the same appeal. As loathe as she was to admit it, doing this with Matteo by her side made it more exciting, more thrilling.

As if they might have been a real couple like the young mother on the dock had assumed.

Now, that was dangerous territory better left unexplored. But it didn't mean she couldn't take this as the opportunity it was. Nothing said she couldn't enjoy herself today. She'd dare to say she deserved some lighthearted fun.

The only problem was, it was starting to become quite difficult to view the man with her in any kind of lightened way.

As soon as Matteo sat down next to her,

Franco appeared with a tray laden with fresh fruit, crispy crackers and thinly sliced meat. Along with two very large bright orange cocktails.

Aperol Spritzes. She had to be careful; those always tended to go to her head.

"An aperitif," Franco said, setting the tray down between them, then walking away.

"Something about all this seems so familiar," Matteo began.

"Oh?"

"I think my parents and I might have gone sailing off this very marina all those years ago, during that visit to Anna I mentioned earlier."

Mari lifted her glass and took a sip of her Aperol Spritz, savoring the orange citrus flavors and mild effervescence against her tongue.

"You mentioned traveling with your parents when you were much younger." She got the impression those family trips had eventually stopped for some reason.

He nodded. "Yes. When I was really young."

As much as she didn't want to probe, Mari's curiosity got the better of her. "Not when you grew older?"

Matteo's lips tightened. He looked off into the horizon, squinting against the bright sun. "The trips didn't end. I just wasn't included anymore. Not after about the age of six. Or maybe it was seven."

Definitely not the answer she'd expected. "You weren't?"

He shook his head, his gaze still focused on the horizon. "Once I grew old enough, I was simply left behind at home while they wandered the world. I was still young but old enough to interpret the implications behind my exclusion."

"Implications?"

"I was in the way. They wanted their privacy, without a third party."

Mari tried to wrap her mind around that statement but found she simply couldn't. He wasn't a third party. He was their son.

She couldn't even imagine it, being viewed as an intruder by your own parents. Mari didn't have a mother she could compare such an experience with, but she couldn't imagine Papa ever thinking of her in such a way. Of course, there'd been times when she'd worn his patience, particularly as a teen. But Mari had never once questioned whether her presence was wanted by the single parent who was raising her.

Matteo continued, "I was sent to a boarding school in Switzerland where I spent most of my days until attending university in the States. Wasn't home much, or when I was there, my parents were usually away. I spent the time with the house staff."

Mari's heart began to grow heavy at the thought of a small Matteo wandering the halls of his large Roman villa by himself. "Not even during summers and holidays?"

Matteo released a chuckle that sounded anything but amused. "Particularly not then. They were too busy enjoying each other's exclusive company."

Now she pictured him wandering those same halls during Christmas or Easter, an even glummer image. With no one to celebrate with aside from employed strangers. She wondered how many of those employees couldn't wait to end their shift and go back to their own lives, their own families. Leaving behind the little boy in their care for the next person on the rotation.

She couldn't quite come up with an adequate response. Matteo continued, somber eyes still fixated ahead. "My parents were very much in love. Right up until the very end." Another empty chuckle. "Doesn't sound like the kind of thing a child would be forlorn about, does it?"

Mari could easily understand how a child might have felt unhappy in such a household, when the two people who were supposed to love you the most in the world only had room in their hearts for each other.

"Any child in your circumstances would understandably feel excluded from their parents' lives, Matteo. I imagine it must have felt very lonely for you growing up."

The way he stiffened next to her had Mari wishing she could suck the words back. The already strained smile across his lips further tightened. Matteo clearly didn't appreciate the thought that she might pity him. Little did he know, pity was the furthest notion from her mind.

"Yes, well. Water under the bridge. Taught me some valuable lessons, anyway."

"What kind of lessons?" she prodded. What possible lesson could be learned from having your parents view you as a nuisance who had to be sent away because they were too into each other to deal with their only child? Despite not having a mother, Mari had never felt unwanted or unloved by the father who'd raised her as a single parent.

She'd had no idea how lucky she was until his loss.

Matteo shrugged, narrowed his eyebrows, as if weighing his answer. "Falling in love that deeply isn't healthy. My father fell apart when he lost my mother. Became an entirely different man. One I hardly recognized. He went from a successful, shrewd businessman to a gullible patsy craving affection. A man who fell for the first con that came his way. No love is worth that."

"I see."

"And it certainly doesn't make sense to bring any children into the world if you're not interested in spending any time with them. Why even bother?"

Mari had to suck in a breath at the harshness in his words. His beliefs about parenting aside, Matteo's entire view about love and affection was that it made a man weak. That it wasn't worth the potential hurt an all-consuming love might cause. Such a shame, really. The man had so much to offer the right woman. Maybe even a woman like herself.

Not that she had really been entertaining such a nonsensical notion.

Had she?

Technically, she was on duty. This excursion was officially a business trip. So that Mari could make an informed decision about whether or not to offer this tour company's services out of the Hotel Nautica. She needed to be shrewd, observant, taking in all the details so that she could help her guests make informed decisions. Which would have been exactly how she would have behaved if the original plan to attend with Miyko had held instead of being here with Matteo.

She really had no business enjoying herself quite so much.

But it was so hard to keep her imagination at bay. So hard to keep from pretending this was some kind of romantic date. Silly of her, really. This was completely Miyko's fault. Of course, she wasn't really going to fire him. Mari would be lost without Miyko and Roberta. Still, he deserved at least a stern lecture about inserting himself in other people's lives.

In all fairness to Miyko, however, he wouldn't have appreciated the outing nearly as much as Matteo seemed to be. Mari had to wonder when he'd let himself take a day of freedom just to have fun. The things he'd told her about his father's behavior and the resulting struggles with the family business should serve as a warning that the man was at a pivotal moment in his life. Starting any kind of relationship was probably the last thing on his mind. She'd say the same for herself. She was still finding solid ground after leaving Boston. Losing Anna had come as yet another blow.

Their conversation when they'd first boarded had cast the briefest shadow over their ride. But now that they were enjoying the refreshments, the earlier lightness seemed to have returned to Matteo's eyes. That lightness grew into clear excitement as they approached the ship. The vessel looked like something out of a swashbuckler novel. Complete with wooden mast, skull-and-crossbow banner and the bust of a mermaid decorating its bow.

"Wow," Matteo said, excitement laced in his voice. "That's quite a replica. I feel like I'm about to go plundering and pillaging with my mateys."

Truth be told, she was rather impressed herself. Sardinian history was rife with pirate tales. Here they could playact at one. It wasn't the only thing she was tempted to playact at.

How easy it would be to imagine they really were a couple, romantically spending the day together. Looking forward to an amorous night.

She couldn't succumb to the temptation of her fantasies, however. Her desires had to remain in check. But, heaven help her, they were so close to the surface as she followed Matteo off the transfer boat, then let him lead her onto the narrow ramp to board the bigger ship. He did that thing again where he guided her by holding her at the waist. The ironic thing was, rather than steadying her, the feel of his hands on her seemed to have the opposite effect. It was throwing her off-balance. She stumbled a step and came perilously close to slipping off the edge and splashing into the water.

"Steady there," he said behind her, his breath warm against the back of her neck. "It isn't time for the swimming part yet."

He was so wrong. She was swimming all right. Her head was swimming with all matter of untoward thoughts. Like how it might feel to turn around and plant her lips on Matteo's, right here in front of these two strangers. How that warm breath might feel as their mouths met. It was a ridiculous idea. And a dangerous one.

Hadn't she sworn years ago after her experience with Trevor that she'd fight any and all attraction to a man like Matteo? It simply wasn't worth it. Trevor had simply walked away from her when things had gotten messy in her life. Just as her mother had decades earlier when she'd walked away from her husband and daughter. Mama had complained more than once about the pressures of raising a child and being a wife while running a business. Then one day she'd simply left it all behind.

But Matteo was making it harder and harder to keep her vow with each passing minute. All these years she'd thought she was being steadfast and true to her ideals. When the true reality was that she simply hadn't been tempted to any degree before. And Matteo happened to be one solid mass of temptation.

"Guess I need to find my sea legs still," she said, blessedly reaching the deck. He was fast on her heels, jumping on board right behind her.

"Off to the islands," Franco announced once they were situated.

"I'm going to head below deck to freshen up a bit," Mari told the three men, desperately needing some time alone to gather her thoughts. Her attraction to Matteo had reached inexplicable levels. She needed to collect herself. The excursion hadn't even really started yet and she was already out of sorts fighting how drawn she was to the man and thwarting off thoughts of kissing him.

She took her time in the phone-booth-sized privy. Splashing cold water on her face, Mari reminded herself of all the reasons she had no business thinking of Matteo as anything more than a blood relative of Anna's who would be in and out of her life in a matter of days. When she finally got herself under some semblance of reasonableness, she made her way back up to the deck.

"Ah, you're back," Matteo said. The sight of him now had all her reassurances rushing out her head. He'd taken his shirt off and stood between their tour guides bare chested, muscular and tanned.

"Just in time," he added, a mischievous smile framing his lips.

Mari found her voice, forcing her gaze away from his bronze skin. "In time for what?"

He pointed to Franco and Stavi. "They're having us walk the plank."

Time certainly flew when you were having fun.

As often as he'd heard that cliché throughout his life, Matteo couldn't recall ever having a firsthand experience to prove it. The day was proceeding in a blur of activity.

Now at the small destination island, he and Mari were encouraged to jump off a wooden plank about eight feet high into the water. Well, he himself needed no encouragement. Mari, on the other hand, needed a bit more prodding.

After the initial shock of the deep plunge, Matteo lost track of time again. He had no idea how long they'd been swimming and treading water and simply enjoying watching the birds and small fish that obliviously swam near the two interlopers within their waters.

Just as he was about to start to prune, Stavi used a bullhorn to tell them lunch was ready. He and Mari swam ashore to find a picnic blanket spread over the coarse sand. A basket full of sandwiches, pasta and crisp vegetables awaited them along with two bottles of rich Toscana chilled just right.

He let Mari pull the food out while he uncorked the wine.

"I don't know how you'd say no to this as part of your excursion offerings, Mari. These guides sure know what they're doing."

She blinked at him before nodding, her gaze drifting over the elaborate spread. "I'd say."

As much as he was enjoying himself, something about Mari's demeanor was scratching at him. She seemed distracted, not fully present. Probably worried about all the work awaiting her upon her return. If he was smart, he would be plagued by the same exact concern. The reality that awaited him back in Rome was going to be a colossal drain of his mental resources.

Yet, the only thing distracting him from all the fun was the way Mari looked in the swimsuit she wore. It was beyond modest by any means. A crop top of some sort coupled with boy shorts. But the fabric hugged her skin in such a way that Matteo was certain he'd be seeing that swimsuit in his dreams for countless nights to come.

As well as the woman wearing it.

Matteo made himself focus on the food before them. Getting all this out in a dinghy had to have taken quite a bit of effort. Mari sat staring out toward the sea, chewing quietly on pieces of the baguette rather than actually taking a bite of the sandwich itself.

"A lira for your thoughts? You appear to be a thousand miles away."

Her gaze snapped back to his face and she swallowed the morsel of food in her mouth. "Oh! I was just thinking what Miyko might say about coming to an agreement with the tour company. It can't be solely my decision."

Matteo put his sandwich down. So, he'd been right. She was focused on the business aspects of this outing. Here he was, salivating over the way she looked in her swim attire while truly enjoying her company. And she wasn't even entertaining any thoughts of him.

Served him right. Mari was the smart one. The one focused on what mattered.

He should take a page out of her book. In fact, Matteo was skating perilously close to the thin ice his father had fallen through. Allowing himself to be distracted by his attraction to a beautiful woman just because they happened to be out on an adventurous field trip together.

Mari was probably taking mental notes of exactly what food had been served and the labels on the wine. He'd leave her to it. Let her concentrate on her decision-making.

The rest of the meal passed in mostly silence. With the occasional trite and quick comment about how fresh the vegetables were or the fruity taste of the wine. Soon after, Franco appeared to bring them back to the ship.

On to stage two.

"We'll sail now to the other side of the island," Franco was saying. "To see the abandoned lighthouse. It's a beautiful structure that offers a bird's-eye view of the ocean and other islands nearby."

"Sounds great," Mari answered, as they both helped pull the picnic blanket up and folded it.

Before long, they were back on the boat and back in dry clothing. Mari stayed below deck again as they sailed to the other side. Most likely jotting down notes about the excursion. She'd probably forgotten Matteo was even up here.

That was just as well. No matter that it left an empty sensation in the hollow of his gut. His problem, not hers.

Eventually, a tall, white-bricked columnar structure that seemed to reach the clouds slowly came into view. Mari finally appeared just as Franco approached from the portside. He explained the lighthouse had been there for close to half a century and had weathered all manner of storms.

Mari joined Matteo where he stood at the deck. Stavi was already lowering the dinghy that would take them ashore. When it came time to hop on, as much as Matteo told himself he should keep hands off, he couldn't seem to help it. Mari appeared hesitant about stepping onto the wobbly plank, so he helped her to board. As a compromise, he made sure to only hold her hand this time. They reached the sand within a few minutes.

"Follow that pathway between those two bushes. It will take you up to the entrance to the lighthouse."

Mari snapped her head in Stavi's direction. "Wait. You're not coming with us?"

The other man shook his head. "Franco and I have much to do back on the ship. One of us will be back in no time to pick you up. Enjoy the scenery." He pointed to the lighthouse and then up toward the sky. With that, he steered the dinghy around and started back toward the ship.

Mari stood staring after the small boat as it sailed farther away. She looked more than a little apprehensive.

"If you'd rather not, we can skip the lighthouse visit. Just walk around the island. I see some pretty flowers."

She bit her lip, considering, then slowly shook her head, turning to face him. "No. I have to go. I need to be able to explain the details for any guests who might ask if we make this one of our offerings."

That made sense.

Still, he wasn't about to let her go up there alone. What kind of gentleman would that make him? What if she missed a step and slipped? She'd seemed off-balance all day. Missing her sea legs, as she'd explained earlier.

He'd be flattering himself if he thought it had anything to do with him.

They walked about half a mile that had to be one straight hill. Not so much as an acre of level ground. The base of the lighthouse appeared in front of them after what seemed like an inordinate amount of climbing.

"Is all of Sardinia this hilly?"

Mari took a moment to catch her breath before answering. "As a matter of fact, a lot of it is. There's a theory that native Sardinians live longer because of all the cardio exercising climbing various hills to get anywhere."

The sheen of sweat forming on his forehead gave credence to such a theory, Matteo figured. To think, he'd always tried his best to stay fit and made an effort to work out daily. Yet this was the second time he'd felt winded climbing up a hill since he'd arrived on the island. It had to be the higher altitude.

It was as if she'd read his mind. "It's a bit different than a gym full of equipment."

Was she making fun of him? The slight twitching of her lips at the corners said that was a distinct possibility.

"I've only been here a couple of days, still getting used to the climate and terrain. Plus, I've never had any complaints about my stamina," he added a moment later, then realized exactly what he'd said.

Mari's jaw fell open. As much as he wished he could take the words back, he had to admit to being at least a little pleased at her shocked expression.

Several beats passed in complete silence.

Finally, she ignored his loaded statement and instead pivoted on her heel, then strode to the wooden door. "It looks completely deserted. Like no one's been here in ages."

Her tug on the door proved useless. It didn't so much as open a crack.

"Here, let me try," he told her. Grasping the doorknob, he pulled as hard as he could, putting his entire back and legs into the effort. Not that he was trying to prove anything about how physically fit he was. Absolutely not. That would be childish and silly.

His efforts eventually proved fruitful. The door eased open with a loud groan to reveal a dark circular area. A winding staircase loomed large in the center of the room. A glance up high didn't even offer a glimpse of the top. The lighthouse was simply too tall and much too dark.

"Yet more climbing," Matteo commented, then gestured toward the steps. "After you."

Mari pursed her lips in hesitation but gingerly made her way to the stairs and began to climb. Shafts of dust drifted in the air. Matteo counted about a hundred steps before he gave up and just followed Mari to the top.

When they got to the watch gallery, he couldn't deny the effort was worth it. Crystal-blue water as far as the eye could see met a bright clear sky on the horizon. The large cruise ships dotting the surface of the ocean appeared deceptively small from this distance.

"Wow," was all he could think of to say. Mari seemed at a loss for words also. It was as if they'd stepped into a celestial work of art, staring at it from above. Matteo lost sight of how long they stood there, simply admiring the amazing scene before them. The clouds above shifted slowly across the sky.

Finally, Mari turned and removed her sunglasses. "We should probably head back. I've seen all I need to see. I think our guests would be delighted to have this as an option on their itinerary."

"No need to run it by Miyko after all?" Matteo asked as they made their way off the gallery and began the descent back down the stairs.

She shook her head. "I have no doubt he would agree. That view alone up there makes it worthwhile."

Matteo might have argued that walking a plank and pretending to be a pirate were top contenders as well. Particularly for the youngsters. Or those young at heart. Did he qualify as the latter?

His childhood years weren't ones he would relive or revisit. He'd spent too much time alone, particularly during off-school days when his friends were back home with their families while he'd been left to wait out the time until classes resumed.

His parents were fortunate to have found each other and for the years they'd had together. But they'd had no business being parents.

Like he'd said to Mari earlier, it didn't make sense to start a family or have a child if one didn't have the ability to nurture and love them. What if Matteo was cut from the same cloth? He didn't want to disappoint a child the way he'd been disappointed repeatedly growing up.

Matteo gave himself a mental shake. Why was he dredging up all this now? The past was the past. He turned his attention back to the steps.

"I think you should definitely hire Franco and Stavi, if you ask me," he told Mari, following her down the staircase.

"Yeah, well. I'm still getting the feel of this whole business decision-maker thing. My father made it look so easy."

He didn't get a chance to ask her to elaborate. An inkling of unease skittered along the surface of his skin. Something was off about their surroundings. The air grew darker the farther down the steps they went when it should have been the opposite. It was also noticeably quieter than when they'd made their way up several minutes ago. Mari noticed it too, her pace slowing. A glance below showed nothing but pitch-black darkness at the ground level.

"The door must have swung shut due to a gust of wind," Matteo explained. He reached for her, taking her hand in his. One misstep and they were sure to tumble down several feet. As enticing as the idea of having Mari sprawled over him was, a perilous fall down a steep stairwell wasn't exactly what he'd have in mind.

"Just go nice and slow. Watch your step."

He heard her humph. "I can't watch anything. It's dark as midnight."

"It's a figure of speech."

"Right. Sure." Her voice shook on the last word. Matteo realized she wasn't being snappy. Mari was genuinely anxious. He gripped her hand tighter in reassurance.

"Relax. We'll be down to the bottom and out of here in no time."

The second part of that statement turned out to be a big, fat lie.

CHAPTER NINE

"WHAT DO YOU mean the door won't open?"

Matteo did his best to summon an even, non-alarming tone before he answered her. After all, Mari's voice held enough alarm for the both of them.

"It appears to have slammed shut. Hard enough that it's jammed now. It was much easier to push it open from the outside."

Pulling it open from inside, on the other hand, was proving rather difficult, especially given the inability to see in all the darkness. He pulled his cell phone out of his pocket and tapped the screen. Zero bars. "There's no cell reception here."

"I doubt there is on the entire island."

"There goes plan B. At least we can use the flashlight function." Setting the light on, he studied the bolt on the door. Yep, it was definitely jammed.

"Maybe if we both try to open the door together?" Mari suggested.

Matteo shrugged in answer, not that Mari could see him do so in all this blackness. Her form was barely more than a shadow.

"We can try," he answered. "But there's barely enough purchase on the small lever for me to get a firm grip. We'll never get more than two hands on it."

He could practically hear her trying to think through for a solution. Mari really didn't like being stranded. Not that he found it a joyous development himself, but Mari seemed overly anxious. It's not like they would be stuck here for days.

He wasn't even going to voice that idea out loud.

"Maybe if I hold on to the lever and you hold on to me," she suggested.

"It's worth a shot, I suppose." Maneuvering behind her, Matteo wrapped his arms around her middle, trying desperately to ignore the intimate nature of their positions. In any other universe… No, he wasn't going to complete that thought.

"Tell me when," he told Mari.

"Okay. Now!"

Matteo gave her a good yank. But the effort

only had him stumbling backward, his hands still wrapped around her middle.

"I need a better grip," she told him. "Let's try again. Harder this time. Hold me tighter."

Matteo bit out a silent curse.

"Did you say something?" she asked.

"Just that I hope this works," he lied.

They didn't fare any better this time around.

"Let's just give it a few minutes," he suggested. "Stavi said they'd be back in no time. Maybe it hasn't been as long as it seems."

"That's not very specific though, is it? I mean, what exactly did he mean by 'no time'? We had to have been up top for at least half an hour. Shouldn't one of them be back by now?"

"They might be on their way at this very moment, Mari."

The light from the small device next to them cast shadows around her face. She looked ethereal, breathtakingly lovely with the small amount of light highlighting her sharp features. And wasn't this a time to be noticing how enticing she was.

"Maybe we should go back to the top and try yelling for them."

"I don't think that's a good idea. I consider it lucky that we didn't take a tumble on the way down. Why don't I go up alone? You wait here."

She immediately shook her head, her swaying hair swinging shadows along the stone walls. "I'd rather not stay down here by myself."

"I guess our only option is to hang tight, then. Give the guides a few minutes."

Even in the dim light, Matteo could see just how unexcited she was at that option. He didn't see much of a choice.

Mari must have come to the same conclusion. With a resigned sigh, she walked over to the nearest wall and leaned her back against it, crossing her feet at the ankles. In the tight space, he could smell the gentle fruity scent of her shampoo mingling with the tropical, coconut aroma of the lotion she'd applied while they'd been on the boat. It wasn't hard to imagine her sun-kissed skin even in the darkness.

He realized she was saying something. So deep in his thoughts of how her skin smelled, he hadn't even heard her words.

"There it is again," she said, her voice a high pitch. "Did you hear that?"

He hadn't. He hadn't even heard *her*.

"There's something in here with us!" That time he definitely heard her. The next moment, she had flung herself at him.

He wasn't prepared, hadn't really seen her coming, studying the ground for whatever it was she'd been referring to. He heard his cell phone go skating along the ground, then hit the wall. They both went toppling backward. Matteo hit the ground but barely registered the impact. Just like he'd imagined, Mari was sprawled on top of him. It took a moment to find his breath, though it had nothing to do with the physical hit he'd just taken. His breathlessness had everything to do with her.

"It's just the wind. We're alone, Mari."

"Oh." Her voice came out in a whisper, her breath hot against his chin. She made no effort to move off him, and he made no effort to take his arms off her.

The small light from his phone flickered once, then went completely out. The only sound now was her soft gasps. His body responded immediately as heat curled through his core and shot through his every cell.

"Matteo?"

The way she said his name turned the heat to scorching hot. He couldn't even be sure which one of them moved first. But in the next instant their lips were joined.

Matteo thrust his hands through her hair, pulling her closer. He'd never be able to get her close enough. Never be able to get enough of the way she tasted, felt against the length of his body.

Finally, a small voice of reason cried out in the back recesses of his brain. Though it would be so easy to continue kissing her, tasting her, pulling her ever so closer to him, Matteo knew he had to stop.

This wasn't the time or the place. With more strength than he would have guessed he possessed, he reluctantly let her go.

More.

The single word echoed through Mari's mind, emanating deep from her very soul. They'd always been headed here, hadn't they? Even that first day when he'd approached her, full of bluster and innuendo, deep in her core she'd known she was being faced with an attraction that was going to take her by surprise, sweep her off-balance. That she was powerless to stop it no matter what she'd vowed all those years ago about falling for someone again.

She'd just refused to admit it to herself. Until now.

Now there was no denying what her senses were crying out for. More of Matteo Talarico. The taste of him, the heat of him. The way he made her feel even when he wasn't touching her. The feel of his fingers thrust through her hair.

It was all so much better than she'd imagined. And oh, how she'd imagined. Even as recently as when they'd had lunch together on the beach.

She'd lied to him back then when he'd asked her what she'd been thinking of. Mari very well couldn't have admitted that it was this very thing that ruled her thoughts. She couldn't tell him that it was him on her mind. Kissing him. Being held by him. Who knew that the very thing she'd been fantasizing about would be happening just a few short hours later? But this was much better than any fantasy. She wrapped her arms around him tighter, pressed farther against his length. She would never be able to get enough.

Not like this.

Mari couldn't even be sure which one of them had spoken the words. But they flooded her mind like torrents of ice water splashed over her skin. This wasn't the time or the place.

"Mari," Matteo's voice sounded in her ears, speaking the words as if he'd read her mind. "This is not the time. And not the place. Not like this."

Heat rushed to her face as the shame flooded her. Thank heavens one of them had the sense of mind to say so. He was so very right. That didn't make pulling away from him any easier. The darkness made it hard to read his features. Mari couldn't decide if that was a good thing or not.

With trembling fingers, she rubbed her tingling lips. "Oh, my..."

"It's not that I don't want—"

She cut him off, couldn't listen to such words right now. "I know, Matteo. I'm not sure what just happened."

"I'm pretty sure I know," he countered, running his hands up her shoulders. "But when we're finally together, it won't be in a dark and damp basement."

When. He'd said *when.* As if it was a certainty, this thing between them.

Her mind began scrambling for the words to acknowledge his assumption, her heart pounding in her chest. But there was another pounding sound ringing in her ears, drawing her attention, coming from outside her head. Actually, the sound was coming from outside. *Outside.*

"I think someone's here finally," Matteo said, his breath hot against her face.

Right. Someone was at the door, knocking. That was what that noise was.

Mari wasn't sure whether to feel relieved or frustrated. Or both.

"We should probably go and answer," Matteo added gently. She realized with no small amount of shame that she'd made no effort to remove herself from his embrace. Not that he'd made any kind of effort to let her go either.

Scrambling for some sense of grounding, Mari pulled her arms from off his shoulders. Her lips tingled and she traced them with trembling fingers. The action didn't seem to be lost on Matteo. His eyes grew darker with heat. They were never going to answer the knocking at this rate.

"We really should get that," she prompted.

Still, it took several moments for either of them to move. When she finally managed to pull herself off him, Matteo slowly straightened and adjusted his collar. Mari's fingers itched to reach out and run her hands through his tousled hair. She resisted the urge. Matteo looked every bit a man who was just interrupted. Mari shuddered to think how her own state of disarray might appear. It wasn't going to take much extrapolation to figure out what might have happened in here between the two of them just now.

Whoever was at the door would undoubtedly put two and two together pretty quickly.

A few short seconds later, the door swung open with a loud squeaking noise. Light flooded through the doorway, framing Stavi in the frame.

The man gave them a sheepish shrug. "*Scusa*, Signora, Signore. We may have made a mistaken assumption."

"What kind of assumption?" Matteo asked, making Mari stifle another groan. She could only guess. Did Matteo have to make him spell it out?

"Well, we figured maybe you would appreciate some time alone in here together." Stavi looked off to the side; he didn't look particularly chagrined. More amused, actually.

Mari did her best to keep a lid on her emotions. It wasn't easy. "I'm not sure what would lead you to believe we'd like to be stuck here for so long. We left the gallery a while ago. It's dark and damp down here."

Stavi's eyebrows drew together, his lips tightened. His entire expression read "the lady doth protest too much." Mari dropped her gaze down to the floor, a rush of heat flooding her cheeks. She could only imagine the deep red color they would appear. Why did people keep assuming they were a couple anyway? The mother at the pier, these tour guides. Even Miyko was intent on throwing them together on this tour.

Stavi gestured to them to step out, speaking as she strode past him. "I hope this doesn't mean we won't get the contract."

This time, Mari did groan out loud. As far as what the last hour might mean, the contract wasn't even in her top ten.

By the time they made it back to the marina and met their chauffeur, Mari's heart had steadied somewhat. But not by much.

The events of the last few hours seemed like something out of a dream, as if they hadn't even happened.

But they had. She had kissed Matteo. And she could have—probably would have, even—gone much further if not for the interruption.

After they'd gone a few miles, Matteo turned to her with a tight expression. "Look, Mari. About what just happened back there, I don't really know what to say. Only that this island seems to have triggered some kind of romantic impulse in me. And you're a very attractive woman."

Ouch. Despite the compliment at the end, Mari wanted to shrink into the seat at his words. He was basically telling her that their kiss was nothing personal. Nothing really to do with her.

"No explanation needed," was all she could

come up with to say. Matteo cursed under his breath.

She tried not to let the disappointment of his words show on her face and turned to look out the window. The evening was growing dark; stars slowly began to twinkle in the royal blue sky. Of course, Matteo regretted what had happened back at the lighthouse. As he should. As she herself very well should. But her foolish heart was apparently much more pliant than Matteo's. Deep down, she had to admit the truth. Because the fact was, she didn't regret kissing him. Not one small bit. Oh, there was no doubt it had been a mistake. A colossal one she should have been smart enough to avoid. But that didn't make her want to take it back. She liked that her mouth had had the pleasure of tasting his.

What did any of that say about her? About the woman Mari had become when she hadn't even noticed? Ever since he'd entered the picture of her life, it was as if she'd become someone else in that short period of time. Someone who wantonly kissed a man in a deserted lighthouse and then didn't even feel the need for remorse despite the circumstances.

Matteo would be gone within hours. Mari had no clue when she would see him again. If ever.

She couldn't fathom he would come back to visit just to check on a small plot of land unless he chose to build a residence there. And why would he do that? His life was in Rome.

The rest of the ride consisted mostly of silence. Mari leaned her head back against the seat, feigning sleep. No words were going to do anything to alleviate the awkwardness between them, so why try at any kind of conversation?

In a matter of hours that felt like months, their car blessedly pulled to a stop in front of the Nautica. All Mari wanted right now was to scrub the day away in her phone-booth-sized shower and crawl into bed. Then she would somehow try to forget the events of the day. The evening sky had now grown dark navy. How late was it anyway? She got a clue to the answer when Matteo cursed again, louder this time, after glancing at his watch.

"What's the matter?"

"That little delay back there set my schedule back just enough that I don't think I can make my flight back to Rome tonight."

Oh no. A conflicting mishmash of both disappointment and joy warred within her chest. Matteo might not be leaving tonight, after all. But that was only going to be delaying the inevitable.

"Not unless by some miracle the flight has been delayed," he added, rubbing a palm down his face. The idea of having to spend another night here was clearly taxing him. Mari would try not to take that personally also.

"We can check at the front desk."

They entered the lobby to find said desk being manned by Lisette, one of the students from the university who covered during odd shifts or when the hotel was short-staffed. Like tonight when Miyko had already worked a full shift and Roberta was under the weather. Mari released a sigh of relief. At least something had gone her way tonight. She really didn't have it in her to deal with Miyko's teasing comments or knowing looks at the moment.

"Any issues, Lisette?" Mari asked, hoping fervently that the answer was no and that Signore Gio in particular had had a quiet evening.

"None. Just one message. Analisa asked me to tell you that she plans to call you in the morning. It's about the gala next week."

Analisa was the president at the university. Though what the woman needed to talk to her about regarding the annual fundraiser ball was lost on Mari. The event was going to be sad enough this year without Anna's presence.

After brief introductions, Mari made her way

to the computer monitor and called up the airline site. The screen loaded information on upcoming flights. Nothing appeared to be delayed.

Matteo bit out another curse. The pirate cruise must have had an effect on him. He was swearing like a sailor all of a sudden. Or maybe he was just growing more comfortable in her presence. She didn't have the time or sense of mind to analyze that possibility just now.

"Looks like I'm stuck here another night," he said above Mari's shoulder.

Stuck.

His use of that particular word struck Mari harder than it should have.

"Guess I'll need the room again," he added a moment later.

Lisette's head snapped up, confusion etched across her face. Mari knew what was coming. She came perilously close to uttering a curse herself, her mind scrambling for a fix before the other woman made the announcement. "But there are no free rooms, Signore. We are full this evening." She motioned to the door behind her. "We've taken the liberty of moving your bags to the storage room. Miyko led me to believe you would be checking out this evening."

Matteo blinked at Lisette, then turned to her and blinked some more. Mari could practically visualize his trying to process the ramifications. "You mean I have to try and find another place to stay? Isn't there anywhere I can room here? A utility closet?" He pointed to the same door. "That storage room, perhaps."

Sure. Either of those options might make sense if he was okay sleeping upright. They were both barely bigger than a phone booth.

There really was only one other option, other than tossing Matteo out on to the street. Which, truth be told, did hold a certain appeal.

She spoke quickly, before she could change her mind, hoping against hope that she wasn't making yet another colossal mistake given what had almost happened between them at the lighthouse. "You can stay in my suite."

CHAPTER TEN

MATTEO WASN'T SO sure how wise this was. But it wasn't as if he'd had much choice.

Following Mari into her apartment with his bags in tow, he thought of all the other options. Maybe he should have chosen to just wander the streets until morning.

Standing across the room by the door, Mari sent him a soft smile. "I know the place is rather small. But it's just the one night. Hopefully you can find a way to make yourself comfortable."

Hardly likely. But not in the way she might think.

Mari continued. "I'm sorry, I know it's not quite what you're used to."

Here she was actually apologizing when she was gracious enough to let him spend the night in her apartment. She could have easily sent him on his way, told him to bide his time at the airport. Or anywhere else.

In a previous life, he might have been tempted

to take advantage of the situation. But not now. Not with Mari. With Mari, he was going to do his best to remain the utmost gentleman until this trial of a night led to morning.

"Please don't apologize," he said, setting his bags down by the kitchen counter. "This is more than hospitable of you. I'm the one who should be sorry about the inconvenience."

Mari glanced off to the side, as if unsure what to say. They were walking on proverbial eggshells. As if they were barely more than strangers forced to share a small space for the night. As if he hadn't been holding her tight against his chest, tasting her while she straddled him just a few hours ago.

"You should probably take the bed," she told him. "You're much too big for the—"

He wasn't even going to let her finish that sentence. "Absolutely not. The couch is fine. I am not going to kick you out of your own bed, Mari."

"But—"

He held a hand up before she could argue any further. "Don't even bother, it's out of the question. Like you said, this is only for one night."

She nodded once. "Right. Let me get you a pillow and some covers, then. I'll be right back."

Matteo watched her stride to her bedroom

and rubbed a hand down his face. Eyeing the couch, he had to acknowledge just how small it indeed was. Barely more than a love seat. But he would make do, even sleep sitting up if he had to.

Something told him he wasn't about to get much shut-eye anyway. Not with knowing Mari was just a few feet away.

She returned carrying an oversize pillow and thick knit cover. "Well, good night, then," she said, handing him the items.

"Good night."

Mari offered a small smile before heading into her bedroom and shutting the door. By the time Matteo slipped on his nightwear, turned off the light and got under the blanket, he couldn't hear her rustling around behind her door any longer.

His mind wandered to all sorts of unwanted places. Was she asleep already? Was she a light sleeper? What did she wear to bed? Did she like comfortable pajamas or something basic like shorts and a T-shirt? Or a skimpy nightie? His breath hitched and then stopped altogether at the next option—maybe she slept wearing nothing at all.

With a self-aimed curse, Matteo tossed to his side a bit too forcefully. In the process, he flung out his arm and smacked it against the center wooden coffee table. A loud thud echoed through the room at the contact followed by another even louder one as the table toppled over.

Mari's door flung open another moment later. "Is everything all right? What happened?" she asked, flipping the wall switch. Bright light bathed the room. She held her hand against her chest.

Matteo sat up, cursing himself silently. "Nothing. I just appear to be uncharacteristically clumsy these days. I'm sorry I woke you."

Well, on the bright side, at least a couple of his earlier questions were now answered. Mari wore an oversize, long-sleeved shirt and baggy gym shorts that hung low on her hips. Matteo's eyes fell to her shapely tanned thighs before he shut them tight. How in the world could a woman look so sexy wearing the most casual attire? When he opened his lids, he made sure to focus on her face.

Her gaze traveled over him to the upended table, then back to where he sat on the sofa. A determined look washed over her features.

"That settles it. You will be sleeping on the bed, and I'll sleep out here."

His answer to that was simple. "No."

She slammed her hands on her hips. "I will

crawl over you and struggle to push you off if I have to."

That particular image had blood shooting to various parts of Matteo's body. Mari's eyes grew wide as she realized what she'd said, and a slight flush of pink spread across her cheeks.

"Mari, I'll be fine out here," Matteo insisted, though the mess on the floor said otherwise.

Mari released a loud sigh. "Look, this is silly. We're both adults. I have a wide bed. Let's just share it and make sure to stay on our respective sides. You can do that, can't you?" She threw out the last statement like some kind of challenge.

Matteo wasn't about to admit that it just might be a challenge he could very well fail.

Maybe this wasn't such a great idea.

Every cell in Mari's body was fully aware of the man lying on his side with his back to her less than a foot away on the mattress. She'd clearly misjudged the size of said mattress. It seemed much smaller now with Matteo atop it. In fact, her entire room felt much smaller with him in it. She could barely make out his shadow in the darkness. The lack of a visual seemed to add to their closeness somehow. Why had she never thought to plug a night-light in? Did she have any in the house anywhere? Perhaps she should go look.

"I'm keeping you awake, aren't I?" Matteo's voice sounded through the darkness. "Just by being here. I should leave."

Mari threw her arm over her eyes. So much for pretending slumber.

"That's not necessary. Besides, it's not just you." Maybe just like 95 percent or so. But she was telling the truth. There were actually other things on her mind keeping it from shutting down for the night.

"Oh? How's that?" Matteo asked.

Mari sucked in a deep breath. She shouldn't have said anything. Should have just offered Matteo warm milk or something and gotten some for herself. Instead, she'd opened the door to further conversation. And she couldn't seem to stop.

"At the lighthouse," she began, seemingly unable to stop herself. Then she couldn't seem to come up with more to say. Several beats passed in awkward silence.

"Yes?" Matteo finally prompted.

"I'd like to explain."

"Mari, you don't have to say anything."

"No. It's not... That isn't what I mean." If he was referring to the kiss, heaven knew there was no way to explain *that*. She wanted to explain her reaction at realizing they were stuck with the door jammed.

"Then?"

"The way I panicked. When we couldn't get out. That isn't how I am. I mean, now. And before I wasn't either." Mari stifled a groan of frustration. Now she was just jumbling her words. There was no use. "Never mind. Forget it."

Matteo turned to her in the darkness. "Please go on, Mari. I want to know. Before what?"

Before her life was completely altered in ways she would have never expected. Suddenly, she wished fervently that she'd never opened this can of worms. Where to even start?

"Tell me," Matteo prodded, his voice soft and gentle, barely more than a whisper.

"I'm not sure where to start, really," she admitted. "I just wanted you to know that the way I panicked, when we were trapped. I wasn't always like that."

"What were you like?"

"I was clearheaded. Calm. The type of person who looks for solutions rather than panicking. I'd like to think I'm back to behaving that way again. Though you wouldn't know it from my reaction to the jammed lighthouse door this afternoon."

"Mari, don't think anything of it. I certainly didn't. You behaved as many people might under such circumstances."

"That's just it. There was a time when I would have kept a cooler head. I thought I'd worked my way back to being that person again, here in Sardinia."

"Tell me," he repeated.

"Everything changed when I lost my father. It was rather unexpected. I wasn't prepared."

"What about your mother?"

She scoffed. "She walked out when I was barely a teen. I came home from middle school one day and she just wasn't there. All her things were gone. It was just Papa and me after that."

"He was a good father."

"The absolute best."

She couldn't even be sure why she was getting into all this. The past was the past. But now that the words were flowing, she couldn't seem to pull them back.

"I was barely twenty when I lost him," she continued. "Attending Boston College, not too far from home in the North End."

"The North End," Matteo supplied. "Boston's Little Italy."

She nodded, not that he could really see her. It really was cave-like dark in here. She'd never actually realized before just how black the nights were in her room.

"I came home weekends to help in the restaurant," she told him. "A restaurant I'd been groomed to take over since I was a child."

"What happened?"

Mari sucked in a breath as the memories washed over her, painful and cutting. In the darkness, the scenes played before her eyes like a sad movie. "My father was an excellent parent and a skilled chef. But he wasn't the best planner. He left us vulnerable."

"Vulnerable how?"

"My uncle swooped in like a vulture. All too ready to take over an established business he had no hand in creating or nurturing over the years. A business I was trained to take over when the time came."

"He pushed you out?"

If only that had been the extent of it. "First he tried to tell me I couldn't handle it. That I didn't have what it took to run a restaurant. I pushed back. Told him that I had to try. When that didn't work, he tried a much more cunning way."

"What was that?"

Mari took a deep, shaky breath before she could continue. "A wealth of earnings went mysteriously missing. He accused me of stealing from the restaurant, which wasn't technically mine yet."

Mari heard Matteo's sharp intake of breath next to her. She made herself continue. In for a penny and all that. "He had enough contacts in Boston PD who believed him. He threatened to have me prosecuted if I didn't simply walk away."

"Mari, I don't know what to say."

"No number of employees or neighbors or business contacts were enough to vouch for me. It was my uncle's plan from the moment he heard of my father's death if I didn't succumb willingly. And it worked."

"So you left."

She gulped past the painful lump in the base of her throat, forced herself to continue. Too late to stop now. To her surprise, she found she didn't really want to. "Yep. Walked away from the restaurant, college, the only home I'd ever known."

"Do you think he really might have pulled it off?"

"I don't know. I was scared and alone."

"There was no one at all you could turn to for support?" he asked.

More painful memories assaulted her. "I was

seeing someone, but he turned out not to be the person I thought he was."

"In what way?"

"He was from a well-known, established Brahmin family. A family who couldn't really see me as one of them. When the ugly business with my uncle went down, he found he agreed with them."

"Please don't tell me he believed your uncle's lies."

"He never came out and said so. But I think at least a part of him did. In any case, he wasn't going to risk being associated with someone who might be prosecuted. Or worse, depending on the outcome."

Another long sigh echoed through the darkness. "Do you think your uncle would have gone through with it?"

"I simply couldn't risk it. By then I'd lost Papa, the man I thought I'd spend my life with, and my future taking over my father's dream. I couldn't take any more chances."

"I see."

"I had fantasies of returning one day and making him pay for all his deceptions. After a while, it just didn't seem worth it. I'd found another home with Anna, after all."

Matteo stayed quiet for the longest time. So

long, Mari embarrassingly wondered if he might have actually fallen asleep on her. Finally, she heard him suck in a breath before speaking. "Don't ever doubt yourself, Mari. Especially not for being human. Anyone would be impressed with all that you've accomplished after being blindsided by someone who should have been looking out for you. And then abandoned by the man who should have had your back."

She sniffled, then rubbed a palm over her nose. "Thank you for saying that."

"It's true. And something tells me you would have gotten there with or without meeting Anna."

She wanted to argue that. Anna had quite literally saved her. But suddenly exhaustion simply overtook her.

Mari couldn't recall the exact moments after her unexpected purge of emotion. Or even the exact moment she'd fallen asleep.

When she opened her eyes next, the room was lit up with a bright ray of sunshine pouring through the high window.

And she lay curled up tight against Matteo in his arms.

This really was no time to dillydally. After having been away from the Nautica all day yesterday, Mari really needed to get downstairs and see to her duties, starting with greeting all the guests who were due to arrive today and checking the status of various operations that kept the place running. Instead, here she sat in a thick terry bathrobe barely dried off as Matteo took his turn in her small shower. It was hard not to imagine him in there, the way his large frame would take up the entire space. His body tight in the small quarters.

The body that was snuggled up against her most of the night.

If she were a different kind of woman, she might throw caution to the wind, throw her robe off and march back in there with clear invitation, duties and consequences be damned. Heat swirled in the pit of her stomach as a flush rose to her cheeks. No strings, no attachments. After all, the man was leaving today for who knew how long. Which should have been a relief yet somehow had her feeling hollow and disheartened.

What might Matteo's reaction be if she did barge in there? She had a hunch he wouldn't turn her away.

And then what?

Mari gave her head a brisk shake. The reality was, she simply wasn't that kind of woman. The other reality was Matteo's impending departure back to Rome. All of which meant her best course of action right now was to get up off her mattress, stop her useless imaginings and get downstairs to tend to her responsibilities.

Ten minutes later, that's exactly where she was headed. When she arrived at the front desk, Miyko and Roberta were both there. Both of them snapped their heads in her direction, Miyko's left eyebrow rose so high it stood an inch above his glasses frame. Roberta was giving her the side-eye with a knowing look.

Mari was so not in the mood. "Not one word. From either of you."

"But Mari," Miyko began, stopping abruptly when Mari lifted her palm up.

Walking behind the desk, she pulled the main office laptop over to her to check the flight status of impending guest arrivals.

"Has anyone arrived early?" she asked.

Miyko huffed before answering. "Not yet. Has a particular somebody left yet? You know, after spending the night in your apartment."

Roberta chuckled softly behind them.

Mari released a resigned sigh. Apparently she had no hope of avoiding the proverbial elephant in the room.

"Matteo simply needed a place to stay for the

night, Miyko. There really is nothing more to it than that."

"Hmm, pity."

Mari was going to ignore that. "He's getting ready to leave for the airport as we speak."

"Too bad he wasn't given a reason to stay."

Before Mari could come up with a response to that ridiculous statement, the lobby doors slid open and a familiar face strode in. Analisa Mangiani, president, University de Cagliari. A petite woman with a perky disposition, Analisa had risen in the ranks from professor to dean to president in an impressive short span of time. All well deserved. Mari just now recalled Lisette mentioning the other woman would be calling. Looked like she'd decided to stop by instead.

"Mari, *buongiorno*. How are you, dear?" she asked after acknowledging the others.

"Fine," Mari answered. "What a pleasant surprise. What brings you here this morning?"

"I love this part of the city. The beach, the cliff, the pathway. Gave me an excuse to come."

"What did?"

"I wanted to talk to you about the international student gala next week."

Mari hadn't had a chance to think about the annual event given all that was happening here at the hotel. Every summer around this time, the university held an extravagant ball in honor of all the American and other foreign students who were attending for special programs during the summer weeks. Officially, it was a party for the students and faculty who taught them, but the real intent was that it worked as a fundraiser aimed at the often well-to-do parents. With auctions, raffles and mild asks for donations, the yearly event was usually a successful moneymaker. One in which Mari always felt underdressed and out of place. This year would be no different, no doubt.

"What about it?"

"Well, I wanted to tell you in person. We want to add a small ceremony."

"Ceremony?"

Analisa nodded. "In Anna's honor. For all that she's done for the university and students over the years."

Mari felt an unexpected sting behind her eyelids. The thought that Anna was being posthumously honored by the university she cared for so much touched a central part of her soul. She would have been beyond honored indeed. "That's really lovely of you, Analisa. I know she would have appreciated it."

"It's no less than she deserved," the woman

answered. "We'd like to present a gold plaque to hang in the lobby or anywhere else you deem fit."

"We would be thrilled to display it. Thank you."

"And you would be the one I present it to at the gala," Analisa added. "I can't think of anyone more appropriate."

Matteo chose that moment to exit the elevator and stride into the lobby. He approached the desk, his eyes firmly focused on her until he finally reached them.

"Good morning," he said to the room in general.

Everyone but Mari returned his greeting. She couldn't seem to find her words. Her skin automatically heated, her body recalling the way his arms had felt around her.

He was leaving.

Matteo turned to Analisa with a polite smile. Mari finally found her senses.

"Matteo, this is Analisa Mangiani. She's the president at the university."

After introducing her, Mari explained the reason for the other woman's visit.

"Lovely to meet you," Analisa told him with a pleasant smile and delicate handshake.

"Matteo is a distant cousin of Anna's," Mari explained.

Analisa's eyes grew wide and her jaw fell. "Anna's cousin? Really?"

Matteo nodded in response. Mari could sense what was about to happen and simply couldn't process how she felt about it.

Analisa confirmed her guess with her next words directed at Matteo. "Well, as Anna's kin, you simply must attend the university gala next week when we'll be honoring her. Consider this a personal invitation from me."

CHAPTER ELEVEN

One week later

MATTEO EXITED THE car and adjusted the collar of his tuxedo shirt, an unfamiliar sensation of nervousness swirling in his midsection. He hadn't spoken to Mari since he'd left Cagliari a week ago, aside from a simple text asking if they might arrive at the university gala together, to which she'd surprisingly answered yes.

Funny how the fates had him back here when he was convinced a week ago that he was walking away for a good, long time. At least until he figured out how to proceed. The time he'd spent with Mari had been nothing short of paradigm shifting. His entire plan, to find a way to have her give up ownership of the Nautica, was now in question. He'd made his mind up upon awakening with her in his arms that morning after she'd poured her heart out to him the night before.

She was the rightful owner. And she was good at managing the hotel. Where that left him, he had no clue. Considering that his own circumstances, and that of Tala Industries, hadn't changed, the situation posed nothing short of a reset. He had to find another way to reestablish the family business. How exactly he was going to do that was a mystery.

Unfortunately, he was still no closer to a solution seven days later. Which begged the question, why was he even here? He didn't have time to indulge in attending fancy parties.

But he knew very well why, of course. This party gave him a chance to see her again.

A text appeared on his phone as soon as he walked through the sliding double doors.

I'll be down in a minute. Sorry for the wait. Just finishing up.

The woman really couldn't help apologizing for no reason. Besides, something told him she would be worth the wait. He wasn't wrong. When Mari appeared moments later from the hallway that led to her apartment, Matteo had to remind himself to breathe.

A shade of red he couldn't recall ever seeing before, her dress hugged her curves in all the right places and brought out the subtle auburn highlights in her hair. Rimmed in black, her eyes sparkled like jewels. Her rich, thick hair sat atop her head in some kind of complicated knot with a few tendrils escaping to flow softly against her cheeks.

He wasn't sure what he'd been expecting but she'd exceeded anything he might have imagined.

"What is it?" she asked after several beats of silence when he couldn't seem to get his mouth to work. "I never know what to wear to this thing. Do you not think this works?"

Matteo had to release a breath before answering. "Oh, it works. It works very, very well." Try as he might, he couldn't seem to keep his eyes from traveling over her entire body, down to her strappy shoes.

Mari's mouth opened into a small O and a pink flush spread over her cheeks. He really shouldn't have said what he had. Recovering, he cleared his throat and held out his elbow. "Shall we?"

She blinked several times before taking his arm and following him out to the car. In a manner of minutes, they were approaching the tall iron gates of Cagliari University. A uniformed guard approached their vehicle, asking for their credentials before letting them through. Moments later, he was leading Mari through a large set of wooden doors opened for them by more uniformed attendants and into a grand ballroom with a glittering chandelier dangling from the high ceiling. The party appeared to be in full swing with an orchestral band playing beyond a high-gloss dance floor.

Mari's hand tightened on his arm. Matteo realized she was tense all over, her lips a tight thin line.

"Large crowds make me nervous," she admitted, ducking her head as if embarrassed.

He didn't get a chance to answer as they were immediately approached by a tall gentleman wearing a dark suit and wire-rimmed glasses. He looked somewhat familiar.

"Mari! You're here finally." The man faltered on the last word as his eyes landed on Mari's hand on his arm, then on Matteo's face. His smile instantly faded.

"You're here, too," he added rather solemnly.

"You remember Professor Antonio Giraldi?" Mari said just as Matteo placed who the other man was. The professor they'd run into that night at dinner. He'd looked equally as disappointed with Matteo's presence then as he did now.

"Of course," Matteo said, reaching his hand

out, which the professor barely touched in a poor excuse for a handshake.

"Can I get you a drink?" Antonio asked Mari, as if Matteo wasn't even there.

"We've just arrived, Antonio," Mari said with a pleasant, friendly smile. "Still getting our bearings."

"Of course," the other man answered, finally deigning to glance in Matteo's direction only to give him a withering stare. "Save me a dance, then?" he said, his eyes returning to Mari and lingering on her much too long before finally turning and walking away.

Matteo had never felt a stronger desire to punch another man in the face. Ridiculous really. It wasn't as if he had any claim to Mari. They weren't even here with each other as some kind of date. Simply together in Anna's honor to accept her posthumous award.

All that aside, he'd be damned if Mari danced with anyone but him tonight.

Mari tried in vain to quell the shaking in her middle as she glanced about the ballroom. All the usual suspects were here, which included several of Sardinia's most well-endowed families and the top scions of business. As nervous and out of place as she usually felt at this event, tonight Mari was particularly fraught with anxiety. Maybe it was the prospect of having to go up on stage and accept Anna's award.

She was only fooling herself. Her nervousness had more to do with *him*. Matteo.

She'd almost turned him down when he'd texted to suggest they arrive at the ball together. But what possible reason might she have given to do that? Tell him how right she'd been about the butterflies in her stomach that appeared when he was near her? Or how she hadn't been able to get those hours they'd spent together out of her mind?

No. It was better to forget all that anyway.

All she had to do tonight was graciously accept Anna's honor, make the rounds with polite small talk. And do her best to ignore the effect the man at her side was having on her.

Easier said than done.

It didn't help that all eyes appeared to be on the two of them, with more than a few pairs of female peepers locked on Matteo in particular.

"Hey, try to relax," he said beside her now. "If you want, I can come up with you."

She blinked at him in confusion.

"When you accept the plaque," he clarified.

As far as she was concerned, that was a foregone conclusion. "I assumed we'd be accepting it together."

To her astonishment, he lifted his hand to rub the back of it gently along her cheek. "I'll come up with you, but you'll be the one speaking and accepting the honor, Mari. It's more rightfully your place to do so."

The depths behind his eyes and the solemnity of his words held so much meaning, Mari wasn't quite sure what to make of it.

"I have no doubt you'll know exactly what to say," he added a moment later. "Now, let's get that first drink, shall we?"

With that, the subject was changed before she could think of the right questions to ask. How did he keep doing that to her anyway? Making her lose her train of thought, barely managing to find the right words to say to him.

Tonight, maybe it had something to do with the way the man looked in a tailored tuxedo that fit him like a glove. The way the dark fabric brought out his bronze skin and dark eyes. How she could see the muscles of his toned arms under the fabric of his sleeves.

It was more likely all of the above.

Mari accepted the flute of champagne he handed her with no small amount of gratitude. As much as bubbly went to her head, she was going to need the liquid courage to go up on stage when Analisa asked.

As if her thoughts had conjured her, the other woman strode over to them with a wide smile. "There you are. Ready to do the honors?"

Mari tightened her grip on the flute as a wave of panic surged through her. Already? She wasn't anywhere near to being ready, had barely had three sips of the champagne. And she certainly wasn't about to slam the rest of the glass down her throat. That would only lead to a different set of issues later on in the evening as the bubbly went to her head all at once.

A sensation of warmth appeared at the base of her spine. Matteo had placed his hand on the small of her back. His heat traveled slowly up her body, soothing her as it spread.

"You can do this," he said softly against her ear.

The words and motion catapulted her back several days to the moment in the lobby when he'd wordlessly lent her much-needed support as she was being chastised by Signore Gio. He was doing it again now, just as effectively.

The man had some kind of magic touch she couldn't explain. At the moment, Mari was more than grateful for it.

"Would you like me to come up wi—"

Mari didn't even let him finish the sentence. "Yes, please. Absolutely."

Depositing her glass on a nearby tray, she moved toward the stage following Analisa and making sure that Matteo was fast on her heels. Accepting the plaque and her quick speech of thanks had tears springing in her eyes as she recounted Anna's many contributions. The moment passed in a blur, but before Mari knew it, she was nodding in acknowledgment to a loud round of applause. Finally, she made her way back down on wobbly legs. Matteo held on to her arm the entire time. Or maybe she'd been the one holding on to his. Mari couldn't even be sure. Analisa gave her a tight hug at the base of the steps, then ascended them herself to announce the dancing portion of the evening.

"I could certainly use the rest of that champagne now," she told Matteo, beyond relieved that part of the evening was over.

Matteo tipped his head toward her. "You've more than earned it and I will be honored to get you a fresh glass. I only ask one thing in return."

"What's that?"

"That I be granted the added honor of dancing with you after."

***

Matteo knew he was asking for something he shouldn't want.

But he wasn't about to pass up the opportunity to dance with Mari. Not when he had no idea if such an opportunity would ever arise again. Watching her up there as she spoke about Anna, the way she pushed past her apprehension, the words of appreciation so sincere and heartfelt, he wanted to take her in his arms and kiss her as soon as she was done. He'd settle for swaying with her in his arms.

"I have a better idea, in that case," she began and his heart stopped that she was about to turn down his request. Time seemed to stop until she finished the statement. "I think we should skip the champagne and head straight to the dance floor."

The surge of sheer pleasure at her words made him feel like a besotted teen who'd just asked the prettiest girl in school to prom. Without another word, he led Mari to the dance floor and took her into his arms. The urge to snuggle his face into her hair was almost unbearable. The way she felt up against him, the fruity scent of her hair, her smooth skin. His senses were on overload. Slowly, they began to move in sync to the soft notes of the slow ballad. They may as well have been the only two people in the ballroom. Or even the entire planet. The song came to an end and Mari made no move to step out of his arms. So he simply continued holding her, swaying with her until the next one came on.

Three more songs played but Matteo had lost all sense of time. To him, the music had become one long melody. The two of them hadn't even stopped moving in between the changes.

"Looks like the band is taking a break," Mari said, her words pushing through his hypnotic state. There was no other way to describe it.

"Right," he said, reluctantly letting her go. "I guess we should finally go get that drink now."

"I think I'd rather get some air, if it's all the same with you," she countered.

"I think that's a great idea." He could use a good dose of night air himself. Maybe it might help him to pull his thoughts and senses together.

Though he rather doubted it.

They made their way outside and kept walking until they reached a majestic fountain in the middle of a grassy rectangular garden. The shimmering lights of the city below framed the scene like they were in some kind of divine work of art.

Funny, he'd never realized before coming to

Cagliari the breathtaking views a city built on so many hills would afford.

"You were perfect up there," he told her, just to have something to say.

Mari stared out into the flowing water of the fountain. "I'd be hard-pressed to recall exactly what I said even. Despite having rehearsed multiple speeches, I still wasn't quite sure what the right words would be."

"You picked the right ones."

She turned to him then, her eyes darkened with appreciation. And, heaven help him, with longing. She shifted ever so slightly closer, her head moving toward his. It was his undoing, the head tilt. Before he knew it, his lips were on hers, her arms wrapped around his shoulders. She tasted like the freshest fruit and the sweetest honey. Every inch of her felt right up against him. Time became a continuum. As did their most intimate moments spent so far together—the embrace in the lighthouse, waking up with her in his arms that morning in her room, slow dancing with her moments ago. He knew then without a doubt that he wanted more of those scenes. So much more.

"I'm glad you came back," Mari said, her breath hot against his lips. Her words sent arrows of pleasure through his heart as the feel of her shot lightning bolts through his core. She sounded like a woman who might have missed him while he'd been gone.

"Me too. For what it's worth, I think I'll be coming back more often."

She tightened her grip on him then and he thought he might die from the pleasure of it.

"And staying longer when you do, I hope."

"Is that an invitation?"

She nodded against him. "An open one. Do you think you'll accept?"

Like he had any choice in the matter given all the sweet ecstasy he was feeling at the moment. He wanted to find the words to answer her, but his mind was a scrambled mess. Nothing but the pleasure of tasting her registered. Were they secluded enough out here to take things any further? He wanted desperately to find out.

The question was answered in a frustrating negative a moment later. A spattering of voices sounded from behind them as a group of chatting and laughing students rounded the garden and drew closer. Mari pulled away and made to step out of his embrace. With great reluctance, he finally let her go, though it was downright painful to do so.

"We should probably head back inside," she said, breathless. The students had joined them at the fountain, now fully engrossed in their own giggly conversation.

"That does it," he announced once they'd stepped back into the ballroom. "I'm getting both of us that drink finally."

"You have no argument from me," Mari answered, flashing him a sweet, rather shy smile.

Matteo resisted the urge to take her hand and drop a kiss on the inside of her palm. He had every intention of doing so later tonight when he finally got her alone again. Along with myriad other things he would love to do to her. All of which involved much more privacy than they were afforded at the moment.

Making his way to the bar, he nearly groaned out loud when he was intercepted. The president, Analisa, stepped in front of him before he could pretend not to see her and ditch the distraction.

"We're so glad you joined us this evening," she said with genuine warmth. "Anna meant a lot to this place. Happy to have her kin join us here as we honor her contributions."

"Happy to be here."

"Mari usually comes with Anna. It would have been hard for her to attend alone."

Except she probably wouldn't have been alone for long. Matteo could think of at least one besotted professor who wouldn't have left her side. He pushed the thought aside.

"It's clear Anna meant a lot to her," he supplied, wishing this conversation was over already so he could get back to the subject of all this talking they were doing.

Analisa nodded. "The feeling was mutual. Mari arrived in Anna's life just at the right time. Made sure all of Anna's affairs were in order."

A flash of unpleasant suspicion shot through his gut. Matteo chose to ignore it. Analisa wasn't saying anything about Mari that wasn't completely innocent.

Still, he couldn't stop from asking the next question. "How so?"

Analisa shook her head in solemn sincerity. "As soon as Anna got the terrible news about her condition, Mari was at her side constantly. Taking her to all the medical treatments, spending time with her. And as if that wasn't enough, she made sure to make all the right appointments regarding the hotel and that all the right paperwork was filed to ensure the Nautica continued to run without any hiccups. And that the university was taken care of as well."

Shadows began to shift behind Matteo's vision. Appointments. Paperwork. Affairs put in order.

Matteo tried to brush off the feelings of dread

that invaded his soul. He was simply being paranoid. Analisa was simply explaining all the ways Mari was a devoted companion to Anna during her final days.

Only... It was all rather convenient, wasn't it? Upon examination, facts were facts, after all. All the evidence seemed to point to one feasible conclusion.

He bit the inside of his lip to keep from cursing out loud, hard. What a gullible fool he was. Exactly like his old man. He'd been so blinded by his attraction to her that he'd missed what was so blatantly obvious. Mari was there to make sure Anna signed all the documents she would need to determine whom her primary beneficiary would be. For all he knew, she'd held Anna's hand in hers to ensure the right line was signed. The one that gave her ownership of the hotel.

Thwarted in her takeover of her father's business, she'd managed to find a substitute.

Looked like the apple didn't fall far from the tree, after all. Matteo had fallen for the charms of an attractive woman who had led him to believe all that she'd wanted him to.

Like father like son.

CHAPTER TWELVE

MARI COULD SWEAR she was floating on air. The pleasure of Matteo's kiss still burned against her lips, the taste of him lingered on her tongue. If they hadn't been interrupted, she wasn't sure where things might have led right there by the fountain. Though part of her was relieved, more of her was frustrated that they hadn't gotten the chance to see where the kiss may lead. The night was still young, however. All sorts of possibilities still remained.

First and foremost, she was going to ask Matteo to dance with her again. Then later, she planned to ask him back to the hotel with her. For a nightcap. And hopefully much, much more.

Exhilaration and excitement pumped through her veins. Now that she'd made the decision, she knew without a doubt exactly what she wanted.

She wanted Matteo.

She traced him approaching from the other

side of the room. Funny, he wasn't holding any flutes. Was he that anxious to dance with her again that he'd forgone the refreshments? A feminine thrill surged through her at the thought. Her feet automatically moved toward him to meet him closer to the dance floor. Then she stopped dead in her tracks at the sight of the expression on his face.

Something was terribly, terribly wrong.

"What's the matter?" she asked when he reached her side, afraid of what the answer might be. "You look as if you'd like to smash a fist through a wall."

"Very astute observation, Ms. Renati. But that's just one of your qualities, isn't it?"

Mari could only blink in confusion. "I don't understand. My qualities?"

He was practically glaring at her. "That's right. Among many. Astute, opportunistic, cunning. I could go on."

Was he really talking about her in such a way? The fury in his eyes directed toward her clearly told her he was.

It took a moment for the accusations to fully register. When they did, Mari's own ire bubbled and tipped over. How dare he!

She took a deep breath through gritted teeth.

"I have no idea what you're on about, but we are not having this conversation here."

"That's where you're wrong," he threw out. "We're not having this conversation at all. There's nothing to talk about." With that, he pivoted on his heel and strode out of the ballroom. Mari had no choice but to chase after him.

She reached the circular driveway to find him waiting on the chauffeur who soon appeared with the car.

They'd ridden about a half a mile when she couldn't stand the loaded silence any longer.

"Stop the car, please," she pleaded with the driver. She had to get out into the night air. She was going to be sick.

They pulled up in front of the concrete steps of a grand church. Mari fled the car as soon as it came to a stop. The building was one of her favorites here in town. Renaissance architecture and stone statues of cherubs along the tall ascending steps. Right now, none of that beauty so much as registered as she sucked in much-needed air.

"Are you about ready?" his deep voice eventually sounded from behind her.

No. She wasn't ready. Not for any of this. What in the world had gotten into him that he was treating her this way all of a sudden?

Steeling herself, she turned to face him. "Don't you think you owe me an explanation for the way you're behaving? Is that too much to ask?" she demanded to know. Funny, she recalled making a similar inquiry of Trevor all those years ago. When he'd told her he was done with her, that her life had gotten too messy and complicated for someone like him to deal with.

"I have a question for you first," he threw out, his eyes still dark with anger in the glowing light of the streetlamps.

"Fine, you go first, then." Anything to get this godforsaken night over with. To think, she'd been looking forward to extending it. To actually spending the night with him. Now, she didn't even recognize the man who was looking at her with such disdain.

"You said you came here to Sardinia after being accused of theft."

Mari's heart pounded harder in her chest. The conversation had taken a turn she would have never seen coming. Where exactly was he going with this?

"That's right. By my uncle. What's your question?"

He slammed his hands into his trouser pockets. "Was it really a baseless accusation? Or did you actually do it?"

This couldn't be happening. Mari couldn't believe the words Matteo had just so angrily thrown out. Didn't he realize they could never be taken back?

Perhaps she'd heard them incorrectly. Maybe the loud roaring echoing in her ears had muddled what he'd said.

But that was wishful thinking. Still, she couldn't keep from wanting to be certain. "What did you just ask me?" Her question came out raspy, strained. It was a wonder she'd managed to speak at all. "Did you really just ask if I was a thief?"

Matteo swallowed before he spoke. "You're not answering the question."

So she had heard him right. A stream of ice flushed under her skin. The roaring in her ears grew louder. How was any of this happening? Mere minutes ago she was kissing this man with her arms wrapped tight around him.

Now, he was accusing her of the very same ugliness she'd been subjected to before she'd left the States to start a new life. And here she thought she'd overcome her past. Had even let her guard down enough to open her heart to the man who was currently stomping on it.

"Still no answer? Then how about you tell me whether it was Anna's idea to hand over the hotel to you," Matteo bit out, his lips a tight angry line. Lips that had been passionately on hers before whatever had caused him to ask her questions so offensive and hurtful.

Where was this coming from? Mari ultimately didn't really care what the impetus might be for all that was happening right now. All that mattered was Matteo had come to the conclusion that she was dishonorable. Worse, that she might be a thief. All without giving her the benefit of the doubt, or so much as giving her a chance to get to the bottom of his anger.

Reflexively, she straightened her spine until she stood rod straight. "That's because I refuse to dignify the question with a response."

The line of his tight lips turned into a smirk. "How convenient for you."

She might have laughed at that statement if it wasn't all so tragic. For some reason, all these years later, she stood confronting baseless accusation. Her mind grappled for a reason. Had Matteo somehow run into someone from her past back in Boston? Someone who had believed the vicious lies her uncle had spewed back then?

If that was the case, why wasn't Matteo back at the university with her right at this moment, discussing what he might have just heard? If he had any faith in her whatsoever, if he trusted her even a little, they'd be calmly discussing all this over two flutes of champagne. Instead, he was out here firing wounding questions at her. Questions he should have come to the answers to on his own.

But perhaps she'd given him too much credit as her heart had grown tender for him. Perhaps she should have seen that he was not all that different from Trevor after all.

No. In fact, Matteo was worse. Her ex simply hadn't cared enough to see past the lies.

Whereas Matteo was all too quick to believe them.

She really was quite the actress. Matteo watched as Mari swung open the car door and fled through the sliding doors of the Nautica without so much as a glance behind her.

For one insane moment, Matteo had the urge to jump out of the car and run after her. To demand the answers she refused to give him. His hand was on the door handle, gripping tightly on the verge of flinging it open, when he finally came to his senses. Chasing after her would be pointless. He'd only be chasing after something he wasn't going to receive: the truth.

But he had received it, hadn't he? Her silence was answer enough, wasn't it? Mari couldn't even give him the respect of saying in words what was so obvious. She hadn't been able to give him a denial. Or even so much as an excuse. He might have even been able to work through forgiving her if she'd offered even so much as that little of a crumb. She hadn't given him anything. After he'd let his guard down and trusted her.

After he'd fallen for her.

Yep, he really was a blind, besotted fool. To think, he'd entertained thoughts of coming back to the island regularly to visit her. He'd even considered asking her to come with him back to Rome, maybe even long term.

He'd considered asking her for so much more. He scoffed as he recalled how he'd rehearsed just this morning how he might approach her about rebuilding his business with her by his side. As partners. And as lovers.

Thank the gods he's been spared from doing so. Hard to believe he'd been so close to making such an enormous mistake. Served him right for believing for even a moment that a true relationship might be in the cards for him. He'd just come way too close to succumbing to the same weakness his father had. He'd seen firsthand over the years how falling for someone could make a man weak and vulnerable.

Why in the world had he even thought to risk it?

Well, lesson learned, and it had been learned well. He wouldn't soon forget what he'd been taught.

He had some decisions to make and some work to do. Now that his focus was back where it should be, he would figure out how to rebuild Tala and throw himself wholly into making the company successful again. And he'd get to the bottom of exactly how much Mari had intervened in the drafting of Anna's final will. He would get his answers one way or another. Whether Mari supplied them or not. He'd given her a chance and she'd blatantly thrown it away.

Letting go of the door handle, he motioned for the driver to continue on once he'd seen that she was well past the front desk and through the hallway leading to her apartment.

Time for him to go home as well.

She hadn't slept a wink.

Images from last evening outside the church had played like a tragic movie over and over through her head as she'd tossed and turned all night, tears threatening to spill with each passing moment. To her credit, miraculously, by the time the dawn sun appeared outside her window, she hadn't shed a single one. Though the resulting headache from the strain of keeping them at bay combined with the lack of sleep now had her dreading the day ahead.

But she had a job to do. And she would do it.

Her resolve was tested almost immediately when she reached the lobby. Signore Gio stood at the front desk, his arms crossed tight in front of his chest. He and Miyko appeared to be in the middle of some type of stare-off.

She had no doubt why the man was here. To see her. She hadn't even had any coffee yet, her eyes still stung and her headache was pounding harder against her temples by the second.

Mari didn't bother to stifle her groan. Not this morning, not after what she'd endured last night. If Signore Gio was here for yet another fight, then for the first time ever, she was going to give him one. Too bad, actually. The man was due to check out in about forty-eight hours.

She didn't even try to wrangle her usual fake smile.

"What can I do for you?" she asked. No preamble, no good-morning greeting. Not today.

For the briefest second, Signore Gio startled and a surprised look washed over his features before he resumed his usual scowl.

"It's impossible to sleep in the room you've assigned me."

"Why is that?"

"There's a bird, right outside my window. Chirping nonstop as soon as the sun rises. Awakens me at the crack of dawn."

Mari didn't bother to ask why he'd be bringing the matter up now, a mere two days before he was scheduled to leave. "And what exactly am I supposed to do about a bird, Signore Gio?"

He shrugged. "That's your job to figure out, isn't it?"

That was it. She'd had it.

Inhaling deeply, she turned to Miyko. "Miyko, why don't you go get yourself some breakfast."

They both knew he wasn't a breakfast partaker. But he didn't argue. Whatever Miyko saw in her facial expression must have told him better than to try. With a simple nod, he darted toward the kitchen.

Mari turned back to the man at the desk, making sure to keep her voice steady. "Signore, I do a damn good job of keeping this place running and profitable. Most of our guests gush about their stay as they're leaving, and they write glowing reviews about us online. My employees seem to have no complaints either." She paused to take another deep breath. "I'm not sure why *you* are so discontent with our lodgings and with me in particular and frankly, I'm beyond caring. I know for a fact this is a top-notch hotel and I'm very good at running it. If you're so disappointed with us year after year, I'm going to have to insist that you do not return. Not next summer. Not. Ever."

The man's mouth fell open before she got the last words out. Then he blinked at her. Once. And again.

Mari fought back the panic that perhaps she'd gone too far. But indeed, she in fact couldn't find it in herself to care. Whatever the consequences, so be it. Signore Gio had picked the wrong morning to test her this time. And was that the sound of someone clapping slowly in the not-too-far distance?

Signore Gio began to stammer. "I…uh … well, there's…"

She cut him off. "In fact, I'd be happy to issue you a refund for your expenses so far and there'll be no charge for this stay. Just as soon as I make a note that any future reservation you try to make will not be honored." With that, she pivoted on her heel and pulled the laptop over to call up his file.

"I have no one," the man blurted out before she could so much as push a key.

It was Mari's turn to blink in confusion. "I beg your pardon?"

Signore Gio cleared his throat, his gaze trained

on his feet. It took several moments for him to speak again. "I said, I have no one," he repeated.

"I don't understand."

"My wife is gone. And my daughter refuses to speak to me. She's somewhere in America. New York, I think, now."

Okay. What did any of that have to do with her and the Nautica? "And the two of you are estranged?"

He swallowed. "Yes. She's upset with me. Has been for years."

It didn't take too far a stretch of the imagination to believe that statement. "Why is that?" Mari asked, merely because she wasn't quite sure what else to do.

"Because I disapprove of her husband and told her so. She's never forgiven me."

The realization dawned on her all at once. Signore Gio wasn't disgruntled, he was simply lonely. And he had a very odd way of addressing his loneliness.

Mari rubbed a palm down her face. At least now she knew the source of all his complaints. It had nothing to do with her. "Would you like to have an espresso with me, Signore Gio?"

The man blew out a breath and nodded slowly, looking relieved. Mari pushed the laptop away and walked to where he stood. "Let's go get that cup of coffee. I think we could both use the conversation."

He nodded once more, then followed her silently toward the kitchen.

Mari counted the beats until her blood pressure resumed a normal rhythm. Regardless of Signore Gio's misplaced cries for attention, every word she'd just said about the hotel and her running of it were 100 percent the truth. Now that she'd had to defend herself, the reality was crystal clear. She did have what it takes to run this place and make it successful.

Matteo thought she'd acquired the Nautica via deceit and not because she deserved it. Well, he was wrong. Just like her uncle was wrong when he'd tried to convince her that she wouldn't be able to take over the running of the restaurant.

She knew better.

CHAPTER THIRTEEN

Three weeks later

MATTEO SLAMMED THE laptop shut and flung the printout of the latest spreadsheet across the room in disgust. The numbers just kept getting bleaker and bleaker. And he was no closer to a solution as to how to keep the business operating before his suppliers and contractors began terminating their services. His father had liquidated every account he possibly could, put their biggest assets up as collateral for bank loans. Both personal accounts and those of the business were completely dry. Each day there was less and less lira to pay off the bills that continued uninterrupted.

Though he was regarding the old man much less harshly lately. Matteo had proved in Sardinia just how easy a mark he himself would have made under the right circumstances.

With a harsh curse, he stood to stare at the

view outside his window. The gray cloudy sky and wet mist settling over the piazza matched his mood to a tee. There he went again, thinking about her. And doubting himself. Had he been overly harsh back there when he'd found out the truth?

Maybe he could have given Mari a chance to explain herself.

What good would that have done? All the surface facts pointed to a very unflattering picture of Ms. Renati. First, she's accused of stealing by her uncle. Then she conveniently inherits a hotel from a frail old woman she met just a few short years before. What are the odds of such scenarios happening under nonsuspicious circumstances? No, the picture was clear and damning. He was only second-guessing himself because he was a fool who still dreamed about her at night. Who wanted to believe she deserved the benefit of the doubt when all the evidence said otherwise.

A nagging voice echoed in the back of his mind, saying most of that evidence was rather weak and circumstantial.

Enough!

He had work to do. The best course of action right now was to figure out how to keep Tala Industries afloat. Once that was taken care of, he would look further into exactly what had gone down between Anna and Mari. He wasn't about to let it go until he had all the answers about whose hands the Nautica had ended up in after Anna's passing.

An hour later, after staring at a laptop screen that kept blurring in his vision due to his lack of focus, Matteo finally threw in the towel. He'd have to change his original plans around. There was no hope of moving forward with anything else until he found out what he was desperate to know.

Pulling out his phone, he clicked on the number for his lawyer. After a brief greeting and the regular pleasantries, Matteo asked the question that had been eating away at him for the past three weeks.

"What can you find out about the property in Cagliari and the adjacent hotel?" he asked, tapping his gold ink pen against the surface of his desk.

"What do you want to know exactly?"

"Anything you can uncover."

"I suppose I can contact a few colleagues on the island. See what they can tell me about the place."

"I'd appreciate it, Aldo. Give me a call when you know more."

The call didn't take long to arrive. Four hours later as Matteo was poring over yet more dismal figures on yet another spreadsheet, his phone lit up with his lawyer's picture. He snatched it up before the second ring.

"What have you got, Aldo?"

"Well, information on the Nautica was surprisingly easy to come by, actually. Turns out more than one financial firm had washed their hands of the place."

"How so?"

"Your elderly cousin was making some bad decisions toward the end of her career as hotel owner."

"What kind of bad decisions?"

"Let's see." Matteo could hear the shuffling of papers through the tiny speaker and the clicking of a keyboard. "She went heavily into debt, made some really bad decisions and then took out loans against the property to try and rectify her mistakes. The place was about to go under and be auctioned off to settle her debts. I can send you the specific numbers if you'd like."

Huh. All that was very interesting, but nothing so far had given Matteo any kind of answer about Mari. "What turned it around?"

"Well, according to the files, the place seemed to start turning a profit again about three and a half years ago. The lawyer in Sardinia seemed to think the turnaround had to do with a change in management."

The final three words landed like hammer blows through his mind.

"Your mom's cousin seems to have handed over the reins to someone much more competent around that time."

Matteo closed his eyes and released a deep breath. Three and a half years ago. That meant the change in management Aldo was referring to was none other than Mari herself. She'd taken the Nautica from the brink of near bankruptcy to a profitable operation. All while Anna was alive and well and still sole owner. Before she'd gotten sick.

That only meant one thing. That if it wasn't for Mari, the Nautica would be in the hands of the highest bidder. And an elderly woman, a blood relative of his, could have very well ended up in the street.

Mari had saved the Nautica. And in the process, she'd saved Anna from losing the home she'd loved and lived in her whole life. Mari had put in the work and that work had made all the difference. No wonder Anna believed she deserved to own the place. Anyone in their right mind would.

"Was there anything else?" Aldo was asking, but Matteo barely heard. He thanked the man through a haze of mind fog and clicked off the call.

Finding out the truth had taken one phone call and he'd had the answers less than an afternoon later.

Answers he would have easily obtained if he'd only given Mari a chance to give them. Only one question now remained: What, if anything, was he going to do about what he'd learned?

Matteo slammed the pen against the desktop so fiercely it formed a divot on the highly polished surface. He'd certainly been right about one thing back in Cagliari. He really was a fool.

No. No. No.

She refused to let the tears fall yet again. Slamming the skimmer into the pool a bit too hard, Mari barely noticed when the resulting splash hit her square in the chest. Given that it was pouring out, the extra water hardly made a difference.

She skimmed the surface of the pool, ignoring the fact that it was already spotless. It had been three weeks already. Time to get over what had happened with Matteo and move on with her life.

Miyko or Roberta could deal with him if he ever found reason to return. In the meantime, the plot of land he owned sat empty and unused. Under other circumstances, she might have suggested all manner of ways that land could be put to use for guests of the Nautica. For instance, as a paddleball court. Or they might even build a cover or roof over it and install billiard or ping-pong tables. All ideas she had planned to run by him at some point before he showed his true colors.

Instead, it was now past time to forget Matteo even existed.

Right. As if it were that easy. As if she could simply flip a switch. As if her mind didn't replay every moment she'd spent with Matteo, including the soul-crushing ones that last evening when he'd accused her of manipulating Anna—again—without even giving her a chance to explain Analisa's statements.

Well, that pretty much told her all she needed to know about him, didn't it? He was just as bad as Trevor. Or her mother, for that matter. And somehow, this betrayal hurt so much worse than Trevor's ever had. Which made absolutely no sense. She'd been ready to marry the former if he'd asked, the way he'd led her to believe before she'd lost Papa. While Matteo had barely been a bump in the road of her life. Only, the bump had upended her entire existence and teased her with the type of man she might have fallen in love with.

The word knocked her cold. *Love.* But there was no denying. In the short time she'd known the man, she'd somehow fallen recklessly in love with him. Mari nearly toppled into the pool as the shock of it fully hit her. Then she wondered if she should jump in anyway, just to punish herself for being so foolish.

Well, that showed her, didn't it? Another lesson learned. As far as she was concerned, she had no business even contemplating love or romance. Not ever again.

She'd been ready to give her heart and body to a man who couldn't even bother to let her explain the error of his suspicions. Ha! It was bad enough he had those suspicions in the first place.

"You do realize it's raining?" Miyko's distinctive voice reached her from across the pool. She'd been so deep in thought, she hadn't even noticed his arrival. Sporting a poncho-like raincoat that barely reached his bare knees, he made no effort to hide his annoyed smirk. Mari figured Roberta must have sent him out here to check on her.

"Yes, in fact I do."

"Yet you're still cleaning the already spotless pool that no one will be using anytime soon."

"Someone might want to swim in the rain."

Miyko merely shook his head. "You need to talk to him," he said several beats later.

She decided to feign ignorance. "Is one of the guests asking for me?" she asked, knowing fully well that wasn't whom Miyko was referring to. "I'll be there in a minute."

Miyko slammed his fists against his hips. "I don't mean one of the guests and you know it."

"If you're referring to that…that…" She spluttered to come up with the right words but nothing matched what she was feeling. "That man who owns part of this land, I have nothing to say or hear from him. Ever. Please don't bring up his name again."

To her surprise, Miyko's features softened and he gave her a sympathetic smile.

"Come inside, Mari. I think you could use an aperitif."

"Now? Why?"

"Because I would like one, and we need to have a long-overdue chat."

Something in his voice and the set of his smile told Mari she shouldn't dare argue. Swiping the moisture off her face, she set the skimmer down and followed Miyko inside.

When they arrived at the dining room, a pitcher of citrus spritz and two frosty glasses sat waiting for them in the corner table.

Though she was near to soaking wet, unlike Miyko, who was smartly taking off his raincoat, Mari figured she didn't want to risk irking him by asking him for a delay while she changed.

"Look," he began once they'd sat down and he began pouring the drink into their glasses. One of the Nautica's regular servers appeared with a tray of antipasto and fresh bread before making themselves scarce. "I'm going to do most of the talking, capisce?"

Despite his insufferable attitude and overall haughtiness, Mari couldn't help but feel touched. He'd gone through the trouble of setting all this up. Roberta had probably had something to do with it as well.

"Sure thing," she answered, taking a sip of her drink.

Miyko set the pitcher down after filling his own glass. "I don't know what happened between you two, but you haven't been the same since the night of the gala. And whatever it is, I think you need to clear the air or it's going to continue eating you up inside."

"I don't think that's a good idea."

He leaned his elbows on the table. "I see, so your plan is to run from this also. Just walk away. Again."

His words gave her pause. "Also? Again? What's any of that supposed to mean?"

"I know what happened to you back in Boston," he declared without any kind of preamble, as was his style.

The statement hardly came as a surprise. For all of her good qualities, Anna wasn't exactly immune to sharing juicy information when it meant having an avid audience at her whim.

"That has nothing to do with this."

Miyko's lips tightened. "From where I'm standing it most certainly does."

Okay. She would bite, if not simply out of curiosity. "How do you figure?"

"You walked away then too. Just as you are now."

She shook her head in argument. Miyko had no idea what he was talking about. "I had no choice. I had to leave."

"Didn't you have a choice?"

"What in the world was my other option?"

"You could have stayed and defended yourself." He plucked an olive off the tray and tossed it in his mouth.

Mari leaned back in her chair, allowing Miyko's words to sink in until they settled deep into her soul.

She wasn't about to say it out loud, but she had to admit he was right. She owed it to that scared twenty-year-old she'd been back in Boston to stand up for herself this time.

Even if it meant facing down the man she'd foolishly fallen in love with, who very well might not believe her.

CHAPTER FOURTEEN

MATTEO'S PHONE LIT up and sounded the ringtone of his assistant. He had half a mind to ignore her. She was probably just relaying another urgent message from another partner who demanded to be paid already.

But ignoring his problems wasn't going to get him anywhere. He clicked on the screen to answer.

"There's someone here insisting to see you," the elderly woman explained without bothering to say hello.

Matteo glanced at his calendar app on one of the monitors on his desk. The hour was empty. "Do they have an appointment?"

"No, but she insists she isn't going to leave until you see her."

A germ of optimism formed in his gut. Was there even a slight chance?

"Shall I call security, sir?"

Matteo rose from his desk and strode to the

door. He braced himself before opening it, not daring to hope. Standing behind it, being glowered at by his assistant, was no other than Mariana Renati herself.

Despite the anger in her expression, his chest filled with joy at the sight of her.

He stepped aside and gestured to his office. "Come in."

Mari shot him several daggers with her eyes before brushing past him through the narrow doorway. Even now, despite the circumstances, a rush of heat flushed through his core as soon as her body came in contact with his.

"Please cancel my calls until further notice," he told his assistant, then took a deep breath before stepping inside and shutting the door behind him.

Mari was pacing with intensity in front of his glass wall. His heart ached looking at her. Dressed in a casual loose T-shirt and denim jeans, she looked even more beautiful than he remembered. And oh how he'd remembered. The apology sat burning the tip of his tongue but for the life of him, he didn't know how to start.

She had every right to call him a rat bastard and then simply walk away. It would be no less than what he deserved.

"I have a few things I need to say to you," she said, finally coming to a stop. "And you need to hear them in person."

"I didn't think you'd want to see me again." A sharp ache originated at the base of his spine and shot upward. Now that he'd said the words out loud, he realized just how much they hurt.

"I didn't. I mean, I don't. You don't deserve to have this conversation, but I do. So we're having it."

He leaned a hip against the side of his desk. "I won't interrupt."

She nodded once briskly. "Good," she said, then rammed her fingers through her hair before going on. "I ran into Analisa a couple of days after the gala. She mentioned what the two of you talked about. Then I managed to put two and two together and figured out why you changed so drastically that night. It's because you thought the worst about me."

Her voice quavered on the last few words and the angry mask fell away for just a brief moment. What he saw underneath the fury tore his heart to shreds. Hurt. Matteo swallowed past the lump that suddenly formed at the base of his throat and scrambled for words knowing full well that none could come close to undoing the damage he'd caused.

"I have no excuse." That was the absolute truth. Only that he'd been colored by his dad's folly and his own insecurities. "If it's any consolation, it didn't take long for me to figure out just how wrong I was." But by then, it was already too late. He'd lit the match and set everything on fire.

Mari didn't even seem to be listening. He could hardly blame her. He had no right to expect her to hear him. Not after the way he'd treated her.

"Anna figured I needed the Nautica much more than you ever could. You were the heir of one of the biggest corporations in all of Italy. How did none of that occur to you?"

Well, when she put it that way.

She wasn't even going to mention the fact that she'd literally saved the hotel from financial disaster. Wasn't even going to throw that accomplishment in his face. If he didn't feel like an absolute heel already, that was enough to have him feeling lower than the belly of a reptile.

"Mari, there's nothing I can say." *Sorry* would ring so hollow it wasn't even worth uttering the word. "Just know that I would do anything to take back that night. To somehow start over. But I know that's not possible."

She crossed her arms in front of her chest.

"That's right. There really is nothing you can say or do. And I've said all I needed to."

Without another word, she made for the door and didn't even bother slamming it after her. Simply walked out of his office.

And out of his life for good.

Matteo sat staring at his wall for so long after Mari left, he barely noticed when the shadows of early evening began appearing. His mind replayed the scene with her over and over like a stuck film loop.

He'd made some mistakes in his life, but nothing compared to the mess he'd made with the one woman whom he'd fallen for. He wasn't even going to bother to deny it. He'd fallen for Mari Renati and he hadn't even realized while it was happening.

But none of that mattered. Because she was gone.

Unable to stand his own company any longer, he made his way outside and wandered along the piazza. His stomach grumbled a complaint, making him aware of the fact that he'd missed both lunch and dinner. But food was the last thing on his mind right now.

Wandering aimlessly for an hour did nothing to clear his head. The images continued to mock him. Mari's grimace of pain as she'd confronted him. The look of utter disappointment flushing her face.

Well, she wasn't any more disappointed in him than he was. Because that wouldn't be possible.

The evening had grown fully dark by the time he finally looked up to realize exactly where he was. Turned out, he'd ended up outside his father's flat. Pulling his key card out, he let himself in through the front door.

The lamp in his father's office was still on, spilling soft light out into the hallway.

He'd been avoiding his father, afraid of saying something he might regret and couldn't take back. He scoffed internally at that. If only he'd been as cautious when it came to Mari.

He walked in to find Stefan typing away at his laptop. His father gave him a surprised look of joy upon seeing him.

"Matteo. This is a pleasant surprise."

"Hello, Papa."

His father went immediately to the bar and began pouring two glasses of his favorite Chianti.

"What brings you by?" he asked, handing him a glass of the rich red wine.

"I'm not sure exactly," he answered honestly.

"Aldo called. Said he's been trying to get a hold of you. You're not answering your phone and you're not in the office."

"I was otherwise occupied," Matteo answered, his mind still numb. Why exactly had he come here, of all places?

"No matter, he's on his way here. So it works out that you're here, too. Convenient coincidence, huh?"

"Why is he coming here?"

Stefan shrugged. "Says he has something urgent he needs to tell us. Wanted to do it in person."

The announcement slowly began to permeate through Matteo's emotionally fogged mind. There had to be a pressing reason Aldo was making a house call.

But he had other things on his mind at the moment.

His father was putting on a brave face, but Matteo saw through the surface mask. "You still miss her, don't you?" he asked bluntly, not realizing what he was going to say until the words had left his mouth. "Mama."

Stefan did a double take, set his wineglass down on his desk and sat on the leather love seat a few feet away. "Of course I do. I miss her every day and will for the rest of time."

"Enough that you risked everything to find her replacement in another woman. One who said all the right things."

"I never sought to replace her, son. That wouldn't have been possible. I only wanted to attempt to fill the large hole she'd left in her absence."

Funny, his father had felt a gaping hole in his life, and it hadn't even occurred to him to try and get closer to his son to help alleviate his pain.

"Was it worth it? We lost everything."

His father hesitated and Matteo wanted to fling his wineglass against the wall. How could the answer not be an immediate "no"?

He bit down on the harsh words at the tip of his tongue and gave his father time to answer. It took a while.

"The time I had with your mother was the greatest gift life could have given me. I don't deny that I made mistakes after she was gone. But I can't be sorry for trying to find even a semblance of such a love again. I'm only sorry that my actions caused you harm."

Matteo could only nod, studying his father's weathered face. He saw now that he could have given the man some grace. Stefan was still deeply grieving. He'd been a vulnerable old man who'd had the misfortune of crossing paths with the absolute wrong woman after losing his beloved wife.

Along those lines, maybe he should have given himself more of an opportunity to grieve as well. But dealing with his father's failings was easier than facing his own pain of loss.

Minutes passed as they both stood staring at the floor. For the life of him, Matteo didn't know what to say. But perhaps words didn't need to be spoken. Perhaps it was enough that they were finally together, acknowledging the loss that had shattered both of them.

The ringing of the doorbell sounded through the air.

"That will be Aldo," Stefan said, rising to get the door.

Their trusted lawyer appeared behind his father moments later. Stefan poured another Chianti and handed it to him.

"What brings you here?" he asked as the man took his first sip.

"I come bearing good news."

Matteo felt his shoulders drop a good three inches. He didn't think he could handle any more upheaval in the span of twenty-four hours.

Aldo continued, "Interpol contacted the Italian authorities to inform them of a ring of heists throughout all of Europe. Turns out the woman who swindled you out of your money was part of a larger crime ring. The major players have been found and arrested."

Stefan's eyes grew wide. "What exactly does that mean?"

"Most of the money was deposited in various Swiss bank accounts. The funds are all frozen at the moment, but we should be able to recoup some, if not most, of your losses sometime in the future." He held the glass up in a toast.

It took several moments for Aldo's words to sink in. When they did, Matteo felt the weight of a hundred earths suddenly lifted off his back. Miraculously, the nightmare was coming to an end.

He stepped over and shook Aldo's free hand hard enough that the man's feet shifted beneath him. Then he turned and enveloped his father in a tight bear hug.

"I have to go!" he said, making his way out.

"Go where?" his father asked behind him.

"To an island."

Now that his company woes were being resolved, he had other more pressing business to attend to.

"There's a guest requesting an umbrella be set up on the beach," Miyko announced the moment she made her way to the desk. It was barely nine in the morning. No one went to the beach this early. She hadn't even had her coffee yet.

Mari blew out a puff of frustrated air. "Great, another demanding guest to take the place of Signore Gio." Just when she'd cleared the air with Signore Gio right before he checked out.

"They've been waiting quite a while," Miyko continued. "I'd get to it if I were you."

"Can't Carlo do it?" she asked.

"It's his day off," Miyko answered with a wave of his hand. "You have to do it."

Mari didn't bother to ask why the task fell to her if Carlo couldn't. Miyko had made it very clear from the beginning that he refused to tackle any kind of beach duty. So much for a relaxing cup of espresso before she started her day.

With a resigned sigh, she went to the storage room to get an umbrella and lugged it across the bike path to the beach.

Only to find it empty. No one was there.

Was this some kind of joke? She was ready to turn around and give Miyko a piece of her mind for childishly pranking her when she noticed it.

A blanket had been spread out a few feet from the water. Was that where she was supposed to install the umbrella? Where was the Nautica guest who'd requested it?

She dropped the umbrella and approached to take a closer look. What she saw only added to the confusion. At least three dozen roses had been spread out on the blanket. In the center was a basket overflowing with breakfast pastries and a capped pitcher of something that appeared to be a mimosa.

What in the world?

Then she figured out what she was looking at. Someone had clearly planned a romantic gesture and had obviously put a lot of thought into it.

Her eyes stung at the realization. Whoever had done this must be head over heels in love to go through all this trouble. Would that ever be a fate she would experience? To have someone love her as much as this person loved whoever he was about to propose to?

Doubtful. As painful as it was to admit, she didn't see it happening. She'd been burned twice already, and wouldn't take a chance again anytime soon. It didn't help that she'd probably be yearning for Matteo Talarico for the rest of her days.

A shadow slowly began to appear behind her and Mari took a moment to compose herself before turning around, hiding the foolish tears she was barely keeping at bay.

"This is lovely," she said over her shoulder. "I'll get your umbrella set up right away."

"That won't be necessary."

That voice. She had to be imagining it. Her yearning for Matteo now had her hearing voices that couldn't possibly really be there.

"Mari." She heard her name spoken softly behind her and squeezed her eyes shut tight. She didn't dare turn around, because then she might see that this really was all a mirage. This couldn't really be happening.

Matteo couldn't really be here.

"Please turn around. I've traveled all night to see you."

Swallowing past the brick in her throat, Mari slowly shifted around in the sand.

No mirage. He was real. Matteo was really standing here, before her on the beach.

"Please forgive me," he said, reaching for her and brushing a soft finger along her cheek. "I don't think I can go back to the life I lived before I met you, darling."

Mari's mouth went dry, the ground beneath her feet shifted. If she could sink into the sand and curl into a ball without embarrassing herself, she would do it.

Instead, she sucked in a fortifying breath, then immediately shook her head. His words were oh so tempting, and Mari wanted so badly to embrace them. But she just couldn't risk it. She couldn't risk letting this man tear her heart to shreds again. She wouldn't be able to survive it a second time.

"I have to go," she said, making her way past him. But he stopped her with a gentle hand on her elbow.

"You would be more than justified in walking away. I can only vow that I'll spend the rest of my life—of our lives—doing everything I can to make my foolishness up to you."

Mari's heart pounded against her ribs hard enough to have her shaking. Or maybe she was shaking because she wanted so much to reach for him, to plant her lips against his and taste him the way she'd longed to ever since she'd stormed out of his office that day in Rome.

Every waking minute.

Matteo gently took her hand in his, rubbed a finger along her palm. She couldn't have pulled away if she wanted to.

"My behavior that night had nothing to do with you, Mari. Please try and understand."

She most certainly was, trying that is. And as much as she wanted to take his words at face value, the reality was that he'd hurt her. Deeply.

Matteo used his free hand to ram his fingers

through his hair. "I'm making a mess of this, I know."

"Maybe I should do the talking, then," she suggested with a bravado she didn't quite feel.

His gaze bore into hers. "Please. I owe it to you to listen to every word you want to say."

Very well, then. It wouldn't be too difficult to find the words. After all, she'd had internal rehearsals of such a conversation between them every day since she'd last seen him. Gulping a sharp breath, she began, "Your first reaction that night was to believe the worst. Your next reaction was to simply leave."

He tightened his grip on her hand, didn't interrupt her. Good thing, too, because if she didn't get this out all at once, she may never be able to. "The way you thought the worst of me and then walked away hurt more than anything I've had to endure in the past. Not my uncle's duplicity or the way I'd been betrayed all those years ago. I need to be sure I can protect my heart from that ever happening again. I don't think I can survive it if it did."

He forcefully shook his head. "Mari, you won't have to. I'll do anything to convince you."

"Maybe you can start by telling me why."

Matteo closed his eyes tight, tilted his head upward. "You came along when I least expected it. And you swept me off my feet. I didn't know how to handle the possibility that you might not be exactly what you are. So I foolishly took the easy way out. It was easier to do that than admit you'd broken through all my defenses."

Mari could only listen, reminding herself to breathe. In. Out. In. Out.

He continued, "I know it's no excuse, but I didn't have the best examples of an authentically loving relationship to serve as a guide. Not growing up. And not as an adult. But I'm hoping you can teach me. There is no one else who can. Or who I want to learn from."

Maybe she was the foolish one, because she believed him. And heaven help her, she could already feel the fortified walls around her heart beginning to crumble. The scent of him, those dark eyes that had haunted her dreams, feeling his hot breath against her skin. Her resolve began to melt like an ice cube dropped into hot liquid. Try as she might, she didn't have the strength to resist much longer.

"You'll spend the rest of our lives making it up to me," she affirmed, her voice trembling. She would expect nothing less.

He cupped the back of her neck, dropped a gentle kiss against her temple.

"That's right, *mi cara*. Starting this very moment."

As his lips brushed hungrily against hers, she believed him without a doubt.

EPILOGUE

Eighteen months later

SHE'D BEEN GONE for over half an hour already. Matteo peeked another glance at his watch and resumed his pacing. As much as he'd wanted to go with Mari, and as badly as he wanted to haul himself over to the restaurant now, this was something she had to do on her own.

He'd be sure to be there for her afterward.

The sounds of early evening Boston traffic echoed around him. His first time in the city and it didn't disappoint. A steel drum band played a bouncy rhythmic tune across the square. The archway he waited under was lit up in brilliant lights like the rest of the city in preparation for the upcoming holidays. All in all, a fairly magical scene.

Matteo fingered the velvet box in his pocket yet again, trying to imagine her reaction when he finally presented it. He'd been waiting for just the right moment and thought tonight would be it. But if she took any longer getting back, he might have to rethink his plans.

Just when he'd decided he couldn't take the waiting any longer and had to go check on her, he saw Mari strolling toward where he stood. Was it his imagination or did her steps seem lighter than they had when she'd walked away to her personal mission almost an hour ago?

"You're back." He stated the obvious as she grew closer. By way of an answer, she wordlessly launched herself into his arms. He wrapped her tight in his embrace and waited in silence.

He wasn't going to ask how things went. She would tell him what she needed to, if she needed to at all. He was merely here for support. And currently, for comfort.

Several beats passed before she finally pulled away with a sniffle. He planted a soft kiss against her lips.

"I got what I came here for," she stated, nuzzling her face against his chest. Her words were muffled when she spoke again. "A much-needed apology. He seems genuinely remorseful."

Matteo remained silent. This was her moment to share as much as she wished. "And now I'm done with that part of my life for good," she announced, pulling away and tilting her head up to look at him.

He lowered his head to kiss her deep and long. When it was over, they were both panting for air.

"On to new beginnings," she said, her smile wide and full of affection. For him. It still floored him how lucky he was to have found her, that she had forgiven him.

"New beginnings, huh?" he asked.

She nodded once.

"In that case..."

Reaching for the velvet box, Matteo kneeled before her and pulled it out of his pocket. "Please do me the honor of starting the next chapter of your life with me. As my wife." Popping open the lid, he held it up to her to reveal the sparkling emerald cut stone on a tricolor band made of the finest Italian gold.

Mari's eyes grew wide and her jaw dropped open. She clasped her hands on her mouth and stood still, simply staring at him. For one insane moment, Matteo thought she might be wavering with her answer, that he'd read everything all wrong these past several months.

Finally, she pulled him up and threw her arms around his neck, a happy giggle reached his ear. Matteo blew out a breath of sheer relief as Mari did a little jump for joy as he held her tight.

"Is that a yes, then?" he asked needlessly.

"Yes, my love! Absolutely and wholeheartedly yes!"

And as several bystanders cheered and clapped for them, under the sparkling lights of the decorated archway, he slipped the equally brilliant ring on her finger.

He could hardly wait for their new beginning together.

* * * * *

If you enjoyed this story, check out these other great reads from Nina Singh

Prince's Proposal for the Canadian Cameras
Bound by the Boss's Baby
Their Accidental Marriage Deal
Part of His Royal World

All available now!

Get up to 4 Free Books!

We'll send you 2 free books from each series you try PLUS a free Mystery Gift.

FREE Value Over $25

Both the **Harlequin® Historical** and **Harlequin® Romance** series feature compelling novels filled with emotion and simmering romance.

YES! Please send me 2 FREE novels from the Harlequin Historical or Harlequin Romance series and my FREE Mystery Gift (gift is worth about $10 retail). After receiving them, if I don't wish to receive any more books, I can return the shipping statement marked "cancel." If I don't cancel, I will receive 5 brand-new Harlequin Historical books every month and be billed just $6.39 each in the U.S. or $7.19 each in Canada, or 4 brand-new Harlequin Romance Larger-Print books every month and be billed just $7.19 each in the U.S. or $7.99 each in Canada, a savings of 20% off the cover price. It's quite a bargain! Shipping and handling is just 50¢ per book in the U.S. and $1.25 per book in Canada.* I understand that accepting the 2 free books and gift places me under no obligation to buy anything. I can always return a shipment and cancel at any time by calling the number below. The free books and gift are mine to keep no matter what I decide.

Choose one: ☐ **Harlequin Historical** (246/349 BPA G36Y) ☐ **Harlequin Romance Larger-Print** (119/319 BPA G36Y) ☐ **Or Try Both!** (246/349 & 119/319 BPA G36Z)

Name (please print)

Address   Apt. #

City   State/Province   Zip/Postal Code

Email: Please check this box ☐ if you would like to receive newsletters and promotional emails from Harlequin Enterprises ULC and its affiliates. You can unsubscribe anytime.

Mail to the Harlequin Reader Service:
IN U.S.A.: P.O. Box 1341, Buffalo, NY 14240-8531
IN CANADA: P.O. Box 603, Fort Erie, Ontario L2A 5X3

Want to explore our other series or interested in ebooks? Visit www.ReaderService.com or call 1-800-873-8635.

---

*Terms and prices subject to change without notice. Prices do not include sales taxes, which will be charged (if applicable) based on your state or country of residence. Canadian residents will be charged applicable taxes. Offer not valid in Quebec. This offer is limited to one order per household. Books received may not be as shown. Not valid for current subscribers to the Harlequin Historical or Harlequin Romance series. All orders subject to approval. Credit or debit balances in a customer's account(s) may be offset by any other outstanding balance owed by or to the customer. Please allow 4 to 6 weeks for delivery. Offer available while quantities last.

Your Privacy—Your information is being collected by Harlequin Enterprises ULC, operating as Harlequin Reader Service. For a complete summary of the information we collect, how we use this information and to whom it is disclosed, please visit our privacy notice located at https://corporate.harlequin.com/privacy-notice. Notice to California Residents – Under California law, you have specific rights to control and access your data. For more information on these rights and how to exercise them, visit https://corporate.harlequin.com/california-privacy. For additional information for residents of other U.S. states that provide their residents with certain rights with respect to personal data, visit https://corporate.harlequin.com/other-state-residents-privacy-rights/.